ESCAPE FROM THE MORTUARY...

The room smelled strongly of ammonia combined with the sickly sweet odor of formaldehyde.

His gun still in hand, Suarez began poking about the corpses for the bandits' treasure map.

"Maybe it went with Howland to Durango," suggested Bert. "This is crazy, we should get outta' here before they cover the back door."

"Shut up and help look..."

Suarez had come close to him; he was afraid, Bert could see it in his eyes. He suddenly seemed torn between staying and searching, and getting out. Bert thought now or never, ducked and at the same time swung his right hand, knocking the gun from his captor's grasp. Bert kicked it well out of his reach and ran for the back door. Outside in the yard he paused to get his bearings. A voice growled in his left ear.

"Alzar su manos!"

Bert raised his hands...

DEATH IN DURANGO

Novels by
E.B. Majors

Slaughter and Son #1
Slaughter and Son #2: Nightmare Trail
Slaughter and Son #3: Hair Trigger Kill
Slaughter and Son #4: Death In Durango

Published by
WARNER BOOKS

ATTENTION: SCHOOLS AND CORPORATIONS

WARNER books are available at quantity discounts with bulk purchase for educational, business, or sales promotional use. For information, please write to: SPECIAL SALES DEPARTMENT, WARNER BOOKS, 666 FIFTH AVENUE, NEW YORK, N.Y. 10103

**ARE THERE WARNER BOOKS
YOU WANT BUT CANNOT FIND IN YOUR LOCAL STORES?**

You can get any WARNER BOOKS title in print. Simply send title and retail price, plus 50¢ per order and 50¢ per copy to cover mailing and handling costs for each book desired. New York State and California residents add applicable sales tax. Enclose check or money order only, no cash please, to: WARNER BOOKS, P.O. BOX 690, NEW YORK, N.Y. 10019

SLAUGHTER & SON 4
DEATH IN DURANGO

E.B. MAJORS

WARNER BOOKS

A Warner Communications Company

WARNER BOOKS EDITION

Copyright © 1986 by E.B. Majors
All rights reserved.

Cover art by Samson Pollen

Warner Books, Inc.
666 Fifth Avenue
New York, N.Y. 10103

A Warner Communications Company

Printed in the United States of America

First Printing: November, 1986

10 9 8 7 6 5 4 3 2 1

One

Father and son faced each other, fire shooting from their eyes. The veins in Bert Slaughter's neck roped visibly as his temper darkened his complexion to a deep crimson. He was livid, incensed, groping for dressing-down words while stripping raw the target of his anger with invective. Just as furious was his son Ben, standing wrath to wrath with him, pouring forth insults, sarcasm, and cursing equal in intensity to his father's, though somewhat more inventive, Ben Slaughter being a graduate summa cum laude of the University of Virginia and his father a dropout from grade school. His son's facility with the language and his own inability to grasp half of what Ben was saying were the last two straws to Bert.

The corner on which the argument raged was where Howard met 5th Street in San Francisco. It was a busy spot. People came running from all directions to watch the show. It was a typical father-and-son dispute arising from a trivial incident, mushrooming into a difference of opinion, quickly becoming a duel of insults, erupting into threats and verbal abuse, and finally exploding into rage. Neither of the two paid the slightest attention to the onlookers; actually, neither was aware of them, so intent were they on castigating each other. Standing jaw to jaw, necks bowed, taut with fury, fists readied to hurl, roaring at each other, at the very peak of hostilities both stopped abruptly. For a long, electric moment they scowled at each other. Then, bringing his voice down to a civilized level, Bert spoke.

"This is it, we're finished. Done for. From now on you go your way, I go mine."

"That suits me!"

Ben spun on his heel and plowed through their audience. Bert did the same in the opposite direction. A round of sarcastic applause accompanied by a mild groan of disappointment sped both on their separate ways. The incident that had developed and culminated in their falling out couldn't have been more trivial. Bert's lifelong (since the age of eight) fondness for Battle Ax chewing tobacco provided the trigger. He enjoyed chewing Battle Ax, enjoyed spitting. Unfortunately, in the latter act, accuracy was sadly wanting. So poor was his aim that he couldn't hit a three-inch hole in a standard-size spittoon while positioned directly over it. Following a good night's sleep and a hearty breakfast for Bert, and a poor night's sleep and an unappetizing breakfast for Ben, father and son had emerged from the Henzel Hotel when his father bit off his first chaw of the day and began grinding away. Ben considered chewing tobacco a filthy habit under the best conditions; his not feeling all that chipper and the memory of the rotten egg for breakfast magnified his distaste. The smell of Battle Ax roiled his juices. When an elderly matron passing them glared disapprovingly at the drool on Bert's chin, Ben's distaste became disgust. When his father spit, missed the gutter, and hit Ben's boot, disgust blossomed into exasperation. He started lecturing him as they walked down the street. His father said he was sorry and offered his well-used handkerchief to rid Ben's boot of the offending strool. Ben declined and continued his carping. Bert took it as long as he could, then began to return fire. One word led to another, and another, each accusation more personal and decidedly stronger than the one before.

Now it was over. Ben marched up Howard Street seething, his fury firing him. Father and son had argued many times before, usually over something insignificant. The cold fact of the matter was, and both would be hard put to deny it, that it took little or nothing to set them off. Their problem was that they were not only from different generations, but also from two different worlds. Bert steered his ship through life for forty-odd years by his wits and instincts; Ben was educated, cultured, suave, unusually bright, and devoted to logic.

Twenty-five years in the saddle had taught Bert every trick in the outlaw's bible. He knew weapons, horseflesh, trail signs, Indians, and owlhoots. He could read the land, the sky, and water, as Ben could a book. He could sleep on a rail fence; ride a hundred miles a day in the foulest weather; survive on Mexican strawberries, water, and Jamoka for six weeks; and shoot it out against four-to-one odds anywhere, anytime, and live to brag about it. He could drink any man west of the Mississippi under the table and lick double his weight in those who invited his fists. He was petty, narrow, pigheaded, temperamental, and childish, all curable flaws that Ben prided himself on standing above.

"And he can't stand criticism—oh, no, it might pull the scales from his eyes. God forbid! He's patronizing, arrogant, mouthy, vulgar, as crude as a dock walloper...."

Preoccupied with peppering his father, Ben failed to notice the tall, slender man with shoulder-length, greasy black hair. He was dressed entirely in black, even to his black Texas Stetson. Coming Ben's way up the block, he stopped short and fixed him with his one good eye—his right—recognized him, and slipped into the alley to his right. Ben marched on, head down, eyes on the sidewalk, breathing through his nose, his ire cooling but only gradually.

"Why does he delight so in embarrassing me every chance he gets? Standing in full view of everybody stretching and dribbling down his chin like a helpless ninety-year-old.

He does it on purpose. Always has. How can anybody so outrageously insensitive have such a thin skin himself? How—"

The world exploded. The first shot slammed into his chest, pushing him backward; the second sang by, grazing his cheek; the third struck his shoulder, turning him half around. As he went down he rapidly caught the blurring sight of a man in black running away, fiddling with the smoking gun in his hand, cursing it; it appeared to have jammed.

Not soon enough.

Two

James B. Hume stood at the window of his spacious, well-appointed corner office on the top floor of the Wells Fargo & Company's express department building on Sansome Street near Halleck. All three of his windows looked out over the sun-washed waters of San Francisco Bay. He pulled on his La Flor de Portuendo, Chicos cigar; his expression was gray, his thoughts mired in the tragedy. Bert Slaughter, his chaw of Battle Ax long since disposed of, sat in Hume's visitor's chair on the other side of the huge, highly polished, clutter-free mahogany desk, his hat on the desk, his gnarled hands clamped between his knees, his head down. The volcano was rumbling faintly; in the next moment, Hume knew, the sound would fill the office; in ten seconds it would erupt. He stiffened and winced in anticipation.

The volcano blew. Bert shot to his feet, roaring. Hume ran around the desk, grabbing hold of him, forcing him back down into the chair, talking soothingly, trying to calm him down. It took almost three minutes to do so, during which time they were interrupted by others on the floor, banging on the door asking what was the matter, and two company officers barging in. He sent one and all away brusquely.

He gazed down pityingly at his friend. "We don't know for certain if it was Rance Cutler—"

"What the devil ya talkin' about, ya some kinda idjit? Ya said Ben said it was; he recognized him 'fore he passed out. He *knows* what he looks like as good as he knows you. . . ."

"He was running away, his back to Ben."

"He don't have to see his face to know it's him!"

"Egbert, please calm down, you'll have a stroke. I know you're upset."

"Upset! What are ya, crazy? I'm . . . I'm . . ." He sighed heavily, his shoulders sagging. "I don't know what, just all comin' apart; that's what it feels like, bustin' into little pieces."

"Ben will live, that's the important thing. That's the only thing."

"How do ya know he will? You got some kinda crystal ball? How do ya know he's not havin' some kinda full-scale re . . . re . . ."

"Lapse. He's not," Hume answered.

Bert jumped back up and snatched up his hat. "What am I sittin' here jawin' with you for? I gotta get over there; he needs me!"

"I'll come."

"No. I mean, I 'preciate it, James, but don't; this is family business. Between us and him."

"Egbert, don't do it."

"Go after him? Try and stop me."

"Don't go off half cocked. Ben will give the police his story, his description of Cutler; they'll track him down."

"Sure, like the man in the moon they will. Ya don't know the first thing about him. He looks like a snake, acts like one, and moves just as sudden. By now he's gotta be halfway to Redwood City."

"Bert . . ."

"Awww . . ."

Away he strode, slamming the door in his wake. Hume sighed and sat down heavily. His cigar had gone out. He was relighting it when the door opened and Lloyd Tevis, president and chief executive officer of Wells Fargo, came in. Tevis's physical appearance belied his eminence; it was something less than impressive. Unlike Hume, he was not a big man; he could easily be mistaken for a lowly clerk. He combed his thinning gray hair across the front of his pate to the right. He affected a somewhat scraggly paintbrush beard. He wore no mustache. He was tolerably good-looking, but his only truly striking feature were his dark, brooding, deep-set eyes. They gazed at Hume through the smoke rising from his Old Judge cigarette in its black ivory holder.

He took the chair without being asked. Hume filled him in on the tragedy.

"I suppose his father'll take matters into his own hands as usual," muttered Tevis. "What the devil do we need with a maverick agent? He not only refuses to go by the book, he spits on it! What kind of organization can we hope to sustain with his sort crashing around like a bull in a china shop?"

"With all due respect, Mr. Tevis, his son came within a whisper of being murdered by their lifelong enemy."

"Rance Cutler—he keeps turning up like a bad penny. His whole purpose in life seems to be to distract those two from business."

"They're between assignments," Hume said.

Tevis glowered, as if the bit he had in his teeth tasted rancid.

"That's really not the point, Jim. We simply can't tolerate detectives carrying on their own private vendettas while they're on our payroll. It's undisciplined, unprofessional, unproductive, it stinks! So Cutler murdered Slaughter's wife which, by the by, nobody ever proved. Whether he did or not, it was twenty years ago!"

"Fifteen," Hume said.

"What in thunder is the difference?" snapped Tevis. "If he wants to run him to earth and take an eye for an eye, let him do it on his own time, not ours. This has been going on too long. You've let it; I have. It's time we quashed it, time we stopped subsidizing their private war!"

"I'm afraid it's the worst possible time to raise the subject to him."

"Where'd he go, hospital?" he asked.

"Yes. St. Francis. It was closest to the scene."

"Did you have to tell him?"

The question astounded Hume and upset him. "They're father and son—"

"I know, I hate to sound callous, only we've a business to run."

"Cutler owes Well Fargo, as well as the Slaughters. We've proof he's held up at least six stages over the past two years alone, and we haven't gotten within a country mile of catching him."

"What he's done to the company doesn't interest them. Their quarrel is personal. That's where I draw the line. By the way, didn't Bert kill Cutler's younger brother, what was his name? Doesn't that even the score?"

"Donald. He killed him, but all that accomplished was to rile Cutler into going on the attack. Neither will rest until he's killed the other."

Tevis smiled icily. "Maybe Cutler'll solve our problem."

If this was intended as a joke, it was lost on Hume. He didn't like Lloyd Tevis; following this wholly uncalled-for observation he disliked him even more, mainly because he liked, respected, and sympathized with Bert Slaughter. And Ben. They were the company's best team, no small achievement, considering there were two hundred and sixteen detectives on the payroll, many of them excellent men. But Bert was exceptional; the man was a bull terrier. When everyone else—including Hume, himself, and Tevis—gave up on a case, Bert stayed on it, often in defiance of his or Tevis's orders, sank his teeth into it, and kept them there until the money was recovered and the miscreants were either killed or brought to justice.

Still, Tevis was right. That same doggedness applied to Bert's fixation with hunting down Rance Cutler, a determination shared by his archenemy since the day Bert killed

Donald in a spontaneous shootout on the platform of the Nutt, New Mexico, railroad station. The irony of it was that Bert didn't even know at the time that Donald was related to Cutler. Donald rode with him, he gunned for him, but since there was no family resemblance between the two, Bert never dreamed they were brothers.

If Hume had cautioned Bert against pursuing the one-eyed one once, he'd done so five hundred times. Ben respected the warning; Bert invariably listened, nodded, and ignored it.

"I think we ought to fire the father," said Tevis evenly, gazing at Hume with hooded eyes. "That'd solve the problem permanently."

He didn't mean it, decided Hume; he was only feeling him out.

"We'd be cutting off our nose to spite our face. We'd be dead wrong to throw away a man of his caliber, with his record. What we should do is give him a new partner and assign him to a new case right away. Today."

"You think he'd take it?"

"I do. His bombast and all the other negative traits aside, he's a pro. His pride as a pro wouldn't permit him to refuse an assignment."

"I still rather we unload him; frankly I just don't like him. He's disrespectful, loudmouthed, a know-it-all, and much too old-fashioned. Old school."

"He gets results."

"He's paid to."

The argument was an old one and always seemed to circle, never to arrive, at a conclusion acceptable to both. Tevis didn't like Bert; it was easy for him to find fault and overlook his attributes and remarkable record of successes. Bert had about as much use for Tevis as a fish has for a pair of boots, reflected Hume, smiling inwardly.

"Why don't I check over the current cases, select one, and get on over to the hospital? I'll buttonhole him when he comes out after seeing Ben."

"Two dollars to one he quits cold on you."

"You're on."

"Great. There's nothing I'd like better than to collect for the privilege of saying good-bye forever to that loudmouthed ignoramus."

• • • •

To Bert's chagrin he was allowed in to see Ben but forbidden to speak with him. The patient was in a twilight sleep. The doctor was broad-shouldered, rugged-looking, well muscled, surly, and adamant.

"He's done all the talking he's going to do for the next forty-eight hours," he said, waving an admonishing finger under Bert's nose. "He's as weak as water. Nobody, you included, is going to put any unnecessary strain on him."

They stood in the hallway just outside Ben's room. He lay as still as death. When he first saw him, Bert could not tell if he was breathing; his heart jumped in his chest and he had to be restrained from rushing in.

"He gonna make it?"

"He's hanging by a thread. He's lost a great deal of blood."

For all his formidable appearance and well-cultivated tone of authority, the doctor suddenly seemed overcome by an air of helplessness. He showed his massive palms and shrugged slightly, as if to say: "Your guess is as good as mine." The determination had abandoned his cold gray eyes.

"How long before you know?"

"By this time tomorrow, maybe before," the doctor said. "He's young—that helps. We'll just have to cross our fingers. I've done all I can."

Bert sighed heavily. "I did it, you know." The doctor stiffened. "We had an argument, it was my fault. We split up. Give Cutler his chance. If we'da stuck together I'd'a been the one he'd'a tried for. I'm the one he wants."

"I don't follow you."

"Never mind. Long story. Ya got some kinda room where I can sit and wait?"

"For what?"

"What the devil ya think?"

"You can sit downstairs and wait till tomorrow noon if you've nothing better to do, only you won't be able to see him, and it won't do you a bit of good. Nothing's going to change. Only the sister and I will be going in and out. I suggest you go home, try to get some sleep, and come back in the morning. And before you retire, you might try praying," the doctor said.

"He's that bad?"

The doctor nodded.

"It's my fault," Bert said.

"Horsefeathers. If you want to twist it around so you come off responsible, go ahead, only don't talk to me about it."

"Hey, you do the best ya can for him, okay?" The doctor angled his great head and eyed Bert with a look that condemned him as a fool. "I know ya will," he added.

"Good."

• • • •

Bert stood in the reception area, looking out through the double doors at the street, pedestrians and traffic moving in both directions. Cutler. On second thought, maybe he hadn't hit Ben and run. Maybe he was still in town. Shooting Ben was a victory, but *he* was the one he really wanted. All gunning Ben down did was even the score for Donald. Then a wild idea sailed through Bert's mind. He caught it and turned it over, examining it in detail. What if he were to let out the news that Ben had died? He sucked his breath in sharply and shuddered. What a terrible thought! Still, what if he did announce it? The funeral would be day after tomorrow. He'd attend, of course, giving Cutler a crack at him. From a distance or close up, Cutler would likely show up in disguise. He was good at disguises. Most importantly, from Cutler's point of view it would be an opportunity too good to overlook.

"That's a good idea," murmured Bert. "Scary—wild, perhaps—but it could just work."

Rance Cutler was as shrewd as he was bloodthirsty, not an easy man to outsmart; if he were to pick up the paper to double-check whether he'd finished Ben off and read that he had and that the funeral was next, he'd have to figure that Bert would be there.

"He can't possibly stay away!"

The more he thought about it, the better he liked it. Mulling it over, standing with his head down and his mind plunged deep into the idea, he failed to notice James B. Hume come in.

"Egbert..."

Bert looked up. At the sight of his superior he assumed an appropriate dismal expression.

"James..."

"How's Ben?" Hume asked.

Bert shook his head.

"You don't mean..."

Bert nodded.

"Oh my God! When?"

"Few minutes ago."

"I'm so sorry." Hume threw his arm around Bert's shoulder. "Let's sit over there. You look white."

"I feel weak in the knees."

"Of course."

Hume consoled him as best he could. Half listening to him, Bert reflected on what a loyal friend he was, and had been, down through the years. Not only friend and confidant, but also a permanent buffer between Ben and himself and Lloyd Tevis. His conscience pricked him with the thought of what he was doing. Hume droned on, doing his best to comfort him. Eventually he arrived at the unavoidable particulars Ben's passing entailed.

"What about arrangements, Egbert? Is there any particular funeral parlor?"

"There's Widenhall and Smithers on Mission. I met Herbert Widenhall back when..." Bert said, trailing off.

"I'll make the arrangements for you."

"Ya could sure help, James. I'd really 'preciate it. It's all happened so suddenlike...."

"Of course. Don't you worry about a thing."

"I can see 'bout the funeral 'rangements and the minister,

if you'll take care o' the rest, I mean the newspaper obit'ary and gettin' the word out at the company."

"I'll see to the flowers too. It's company policy to provide a floral wreath. Any particular type of flowers you prefer, or that Ben liked?"

"He liked 'em all, just as long as they smelled good." Bert shook his head and sighed dramatically. Hume clapped a reassuring hand on his shoulder.

"I'll get it into the newspapers too."

"If ya wouldn't mind." Bert stood up. "I'll go see Widenhall, then I'll head back to the hotel and try to sleep a little. I feel weak all over."

"It's to be expected. It's a heavy blow, my friend."

"Ben..." Bert started to say.

"He was a fine son, Egbert. You had every right to be as proud as you were. I... confess, being a bachelor like I am, that I've always envied you Ben. I can't help feeling like I've lost my favorite nephew."

"I 'preciate that good thought, James. Ben would, too, I know."

"Let me walk you over to the funeral parlor. While you're there I'll make the rounds of the newspapers."

• • • •

"A fake funeral?"

"That's what I said. He's hurtin' bad, but he's as strong as a horse. He'll recover okay."

Herbert Widenhall looked properly alarmed. If humans resemble different creatures, Bert thought, a sparrow came to mind in Widenhall's presence. He fidgeted and twitched and was beady-eyed like a bird. He was small and bony but for his well-nourished paunch. He blinked continuously and shifted his head around on the skinny anchor of his neck. Bert's suggestion clearly ruffled his feathers, threatening his solemn and respected calling with all the attributes of a carnival.

Bert explained in detail, describing Rance Cutler as a murdering swine, the devil in human form, and stressed the fact that he was prepared to offer himself as live bait to trap Cutler.

"It sounds frightfully dangerous," sputtered Widenhall.

"Only to me."

"What about my pallbearers? The minister? The mourners?"

"Nothing'll happen to them, cross my heart. He's not interested in anybody but yours truly. The thing of it is, he thinks he's killed Ben, so it's just common sense that the funeral'll follow, right? And even more commonsense that I'll be there, so he's bound to show. If everythin' works out smooth, I'll get the drop on him and take him without firin' a shot."

"If . . ."

"Okay, when. Let's talk money. What do you get for the box boys?"

"Pallbearers. Usually three dollars a man—that is, for a bona fide funeral. Needless to say, all our funerals are. I've been in this business for twenty-seven years—"

"Yeah, yeah, look, I'll pay 'em ten bucks a head."

"Ten? That's forty dollars!"

"Money's no object. Whatever the preacher gets, I'll pay him double. And like I say, nobody's gonna get hurt, so there's no need to tell 'em what's goin' on."

"I can scarcely avoid it, not ethically I can't. Frankly I'll be amazed if everybody doesn't get hurt! See here, all I can do is broach the thing to my people. If they like the money well enough to run the risk, that's their business. The same goes for the minister. I confess, ten dollars is quite a substantial sum."

"Just make sure they promise to keep it under their hats. If word leaks out that the whole thing's rigged, that it's a sham, it'll blow up in our faces. How much for the coffin, keepin' in mind there won't be anybody in it and you'll get it back 'thout a scratch soon as we're done."

"Full of bullet holes is more like it."

"Brother, you are a pes'mist!"

"I'm merely being practical."

Bert got out his wallet. "I'll give ya twenty bucks cash just to set it up. All ya got to do is 'range things. Ya don't have to go to the cemetery, don't have to do anything else...."

"What about the grave? It's customary to have it dug in preparation to receive the coffin."

"That's true. So check out the cemetery, find us a afternoon funeral, and we'll do ours in the mornin' and use their hole."

"Good grief, you're serious!"

"Never more. Here's a extra ten bucks for yer trouble. I re'lize I'm sorta' wipin' my boots on your sens'tivities. That's thirty cash money for what amounts to no more'n a hour's work."

Widenhall sighed sufferingly. "I'll do my best. The rental for the coffin is three dollars."

"I just give ya thirty! Oh, for..." He counted out three additional dollars.

"Did you have any particular model in mind?"

"You pick it out. I gotta run, I got things to do. Hey, if a phony obit'ary's put in the papers and the doc reads about it, can he put the damper on it?"

"Anyone can."

"But it'd take a day or so for the paper to print a...a..."

"Retraction. I'd say so. Mr. Slaughter, don't you feel you're getting in a bit over your head? It all seems frightfully complicated."

"It's not. It's just a put-up job to sucker Cutler into showin'. I don't care if the whole shebang falls apart at the graveside, just as long as he's there. And for the last time, stop worryin' 'bout your people gettin' hurt. It's not gonna happen. I won't let it. I'm the one he's after, nobody else. If you do your job and it all works out, there'll be a bonus in it for ya."

Widenhall brightened. "Oh?"

"You betcha, this is gonna turn out the most profitable funeral you ever staged for hardly liftin' your little finger."

"What sort of bonus?"

"Money."

"How much?"

"I'll decide when we're all wrapped up. So long for now."

Three

By noon the next day, Ben's condition had improved "remarkably," according to his doctor. In the meantime the arrangements for his funeral were completed. Hume got the obituary into the morning *Call*, the *Examiner*, the *Bulletin*, *Chronicle*, and *Evening Post*, as well as the German-language *California Demokrat*.

All Bert had to do now was wait for the funeral. It was scheduled for ten-thirty the following morning. More than two hundred employees led by James B. Hume and Lloyd Tevis came from Wells Fargo; the company rewarded Ben's service to it with a seven-foot-tall horseshoe of red and white roses. The funeral procession rolled down Mission Street, crossed Geneva, and passed Alice Chalmers Park to the cemetery. A number of natives unacquainted with either Slaughter, but with nothing better to do with their morning, were waiting by the grave. Bert had no idea whose grave it actually was. Reporters and photographers from all the newspapers also showed up.

Bert had ridden out in the hearse with the empty coffin in the back. James Hume and Lloyd Tevis approached him near the grave. Tevis offered his hand.

"My deepest sympathies, *Egg*-bert," he said solemnly.

Bert did not like his Christian name; he didn't mind Hume calling him by it but couldn't stand Tevis doing so. His deliberate emphasis on the first syllable galled Bert. Recognizing this, Tevis never addressed him otherwise. Bert was tempted to bark at him when he did so this time, but the situation was ill suited to any but words of condolence and gratitude for their expression.

"Thanks," he said tightly. He looked around them. "Some turnout, eh?"

His comment slightly but perceptibly jarred both Tevis and Hume. He took no notice of their reactions. His attention had wandered to the press corps, one of the photographers in particular. The day was gray, threatening a downpour, and he was the only man in the group wearing dark glasses. Cutler had to wear something to cover his missing eye; dark glasses were evidently the best he could come up with, reflected Bert. As he studied him the man turned toward him, bringing his camera around. It hung from his neck at belly level by a leather strap, and the bellows was out and ready to shoot.

Shoot me, decided Bert. Fortunately a good thirty yards separated them, and people in attendance passed continually back and forth between. Bert walked away from Hume and Tevis to the edge of the gathering and looked down the hill at the long line of various types of vehicles stretching clear to the iron gate and the road just beyond it. Four horses were tied at various spots. One was Cutler's, he decided, which suggested that he was probably planning on shooting him then, taking advantage of the shock and amazement of the crowd, running down the hill, through the gate, and to his mount. But if anybody in the crowd besides him was carrying a gun, mused Bert, Cutler could speedily find himself a moving target. If he *was* Cutler, he'd hold off until after the ceremony, when the minister said his final words, closed his bible, and everyone trooped back down to their vehicles. If he *was* Cutler, he'd follow him down at a safe distance, wait until both got close to the gate or even outside, then open up.

Yes, that'd be exactly the way he'd work it. And yes, he definitely had a six-gun concealed inside his camera. Apart from his dark glasses, his hair was cut short, in marked contrast to his usual shoulder-length style. But his height, build, and posture were right, and the dark glasses were a dead giveaway.

The minister took his place at the head of the grave as the pallbearers set the coffin down beside it and removed their hats. The well-wishers gathered around, the reporters and photographers keeping a respectful distance. Bert made very sure that he, Hume, and Tevis stood inside the crowd, placing at least five backs between his own and Cutler's lethal camera. The minister cleared his throat and was about to begin when a shot rang out. As one, the crowd turned, men shouting, women screaming.

The source of the sound was immediately apparent. Cutler had accidentally fired his camera. The bullet had winged harmlessly away; smoke curled from the lens housing. Two reporters lunged to seize him, but he squirmed free and started down the hill.

"It's Cutler!" boomed Bert. "Don't let him get away! Grab him!"

He bulled his way laboriously out of the crowd, but by the time he got clear, Cutler had reached the gate and was swinging it wide. A dozen people were hot after him, but hearing Bert's insistent shouting, ignoring his pursuers, he turned, raised his camera, and emptied it at Bert. Bert hurled himself to the ground. Others in the crowd did also; still others turned and ran. A large, heavyset man tripped over the coffin in his haste, knocking it on its side. The lid flew open.

"It's empty!" burst out Tevis. "The coffin's empty!"

Bert could hear Tevis's voice behind him but did not turn to look. He had his gun out and was chasing down the hill after Cutler, readying to fire as he ran but holding up for fear of hitting one or another newspaper man running ahead.

Cutler, meanwhile, had emptied his gun and pulled it out of the camera, dumping the camera and running for his horse.

By the time Bert got to the gate, Cutler was barreling down the road, heading for Daly City. Bert snatched up the reins of the first horse he came to, but when he mounted, it bucked sharply and threw him. He landed hard on his rear and sat, braced by his arms, watching the animal gallop off. He began to curse. By now Cutler was well out of sight, his dust piling into the gray sky. People milled around Bert, their eyes questioning. Hume and Tevis came puffing up.

"The coffin's empty!" boomed Tevis.

"Egbert, what the devil . . . ?" began Hume.

"Help me up, wouldja, I think I busted my tailbone!"

Hume helped him, groaning, to his feet.

"Cutler, that's who that was, wasn't it!" fumed Tevis. "It was! You rigged this whole farce, dragged us all here in the belief that your boy had gone to his maker. It was a trick! You used us! Used Wells Fargo!"

"Oh, shut up—"

"This is the last straw! You're fired! Both of you!"

"I quit."

"Gentlemen, gentlemen," Hume said, groaning, "control yourselves. Let's not be hasty—"

"You heard what I said!" Tevis flared. "We're going back to the office, and the first thing you'll do is make out this grubby scoundrel's pink slip, two pink slips! You're finished with Wells Fargo, Slaughter, done for!"

"That suits me perfect, ya scrawny little wharf rat, two-faced, double-dealin', connivin' scum!"

"Egbert!"

"Get away from me, the two o' ya! He's got away, and I'm goin' after him. I'll catch him and punch his ticket if it's the last thing I do! And Wells Fargo, you two, and everybody can go pound sand!"

Four

Bert could kick himself. Not for losing Cutler—that couldn't be helped. And as frustrating as losing him always was, he had long ago become used to finding him and falling short of finishing him at showdown time. He could kick himself for not quitting the company fifteen years ago. Had he done so he would have long since caught up with the one-eyed one and punched his ticket, and Ben would never have joined Wells Fargo, another long-standing irritation Bert had put up with. The boy was too smart, too capable, and with too much to offer the world to fritter his life away for Lloyd Tevis's autograph on a check. Why he should risk his life for nickels and dimes, chasing about the territories, gunning down and being gunned down by owl hoots was beyond Bert. For someone as ill educated, rough-edged, and out of touch with civilization as Bert, however, it was the ideal job.

One he really should have quit fifteen years ago.

"Better late than never...."

He saw no sense in trying to catch up with Cutler on the Daly City road. He knew what he was wearing, that he was riding a chestnut gelding with a blaze on its forehead, a common enough horse, and that he was probably heading south all the way. Chasing him so long had taught Bert a lot about him, not a few things Cutler would have wished he didn't know. Bert knew that he had a strong dislike for cities and a fondness for Mexico. That he would head there was a strong possibility; where specifically in Mexico was the problem. He could cross over anywhere from San Luis Rio Colorado east to Brownsville, Texas, but somewhere between San Luis and Sonoita seemed the best bet. Tijuana was out: too loud and loose, wide-open, and too many gringos looking for border jumpers. From past experience he knew that whenever Cutler fled to Mexico, he headed for country well below the border and avoided the coasts in favor of the interior. Monterey might be a good bet, perhaps Torreón.

Might. Perhaps. He was kidding himself. It was better than seven hundred miles from San Francisco to Yuma just this side of the border. What in the wide world made him wishfully think Cutler would head for Mexico, anyway? Why wouldn't he double back and head north? Or east? Idaho was lovely this time of year.

He saw one element in his favor: For the first time ever he could now devote himself full-time to the chase. No need to play at his Wells Fargo job with his left hand while he tracked Cutler; no need for deception, phony telegrams, double-talking James Hume, or Ben's covering for him, assistance frequently refused and only reluctantly given when it was. Cutler now had the full focus of his attention. He could take his time, trail him patiently; somewhere he'd catch up with him. Unless he left the country—little chance of that. The best way would be to track him in the blind, buttonhole people along the way until the trail dried up, then start fresh in another direction. It was tedious work, but while he pursued it he would keep an eye on the newspapers. Whenever Cutler ran short of money, he ran into crime. He rarely made the papers by name, but his appearance was distinctive, and every time a witness described the holdup man or killer as rangy, dark like an Indian, and with only one eye, Bert could be sure who it was.

Sometimes the grapevine came in handy: People "heard" Cutler was heading here or there, joining this bunch or that. It was a big continent, but it wouldn't be quite as hard as looking for a needle in a haystack. This "needle" looked one of a kind, and people who ran into him never forgot him.

He hitched a ride with a reporter back to town, promising him the true story in exchange for the transportation. He resolved to avoid Herbert Widenhall for fear the undertaker would pressure him for his bonus in spite of the chaotic outcome of the proceedings. Widenhall had fulfilled his end of their deal but, rationalized Bert, he'd overpaid him to start with. He promised the reporter, who was the *Examiner* man, that he'd drop around the office and answer all his questions. Give him a scoop. The man all bug begged him for the lowdown on the way in, but Bert held his peace, claiming he was too concerned over Ben to grant an interview right away.

He had, of course, no intention of telling all to any newspaper. Tevis deserved it, but he could not bring himself to rub salt in James Hume's wound. He felt sorry about Hume. He'd used him disgracefully; he owed him. One day he'd balance the books somehow.

He went straight to St. Francis hospital. He sneaked past the receptionist and up the stairs. Ben's doctor came up just as he was about to enter the room.

"Just the man I want to see. What's his obituary doing in all the papers? And a phony funeral?"

"Search me. I don't know the first thing 'bout either."

"Then who *is* responsible?" the doctor demanded.

"Maybe some practical joker. How's he doin'?"

"Great, considering. Tell me the truth, what's it all about?"

"I don't know. Must be some reporter's bright idea; ya know how they're all the time whippin' up stories outta whole cloth. Somebody at Wells Fargo maybe got wind he died or figgered he did. Ya know how rumors fly 'round."

"It takes somebody to start 'em."

"Not me."

"You went to the funeral..."

"In a pig's eye. I just come from church. Look, I'm in kinda a rush. Can I go in? I won't be more'n five minutes, honest."

"You won't be more than two. He's still weak. He could use blood; what do you say, how about a pint?"

"Ya mean stick a needle in me?"

"He's your son."

"I know, I know. Okay. I guess..."

"Guess?"

"Okay, I said, only I do hate and despise needles."

They talked while the transfusion apparatus was prepared outside the door. The doctor was right: Ben was still very weak. He looked pale, very drawn; it seemed to Bert that he could hardly lift his eyelids.

"I'm gonna be goin' away for a while, son..."

"After Cutler"

"Oh, no, nothin' like that. He's long gone."

"Liar. Bert, you can't. I can spot it every time. Whenever you lie, your eyes roll up in your head."

"They do not."

"You're lying now. Be smart, be practical. If you don't want to sit around twiddling your thumbs and fidgeting, go to James Hume and get an assignment, something in the area, hopefully. It'll keep you occupied. In the meantime I'll be recovering. In a few weeks we'll be back in harness together. Talk it over with him, see what he thinks."

"Okay."

"No you don't."

"What now?"

"That was too fast, you're too agreeable. Bert, in God's name forget Cutler. Tell you what, you put him on the shelf until I'm back on my feet, and next time we cross paths with him, I promise you we'll drop whatever we're doing and collar him once and for all."

"Deal."

"Liar."

"Boy, you sure have some high 'pinion o' your old man."

"The highest. That's why I don't want to see him get his head chopped off."

A table was brought in and set beside the patient's bed. The transfusion apparatus consisted of a curious-looking tube about two and a half feet long with a bulb in the center of it, a smaller bulb at one end, and a suction cup with a shorter tube that was placed in a round glass vessel about four inches deep. The opposite end of the tube was fitted with a needle. Bert was given a chair.

"Take off your shirt and undershirt," said the doctor.

A tourniquet was wrapped around Bert's arm just below the shoulder. The doctor tightened it with one hand while he located the vein he wanted with the other. Bert sighed audibly. He closed his eyes when the needle was inserted into the vein. He felt only the slightest prick. The procedure took about twenty minutes. When it was all over, he felt slightly dizzy, and when he stood up to put his undershirt and shirt back on, the room seemed to tilt under his feet.

"Sit back down and stay down till you get your bearings. The dizziness'll pass."

"What dizziness? I'm fit as a fiddle."

A glass of orange juice was brought to him and he drank it. Ben had fallen asleep. Bert imagined he saw his blood already working, restoring, however slightly, a bit of color to Ben's cheeks.

"Good-bye, son, wish your old man luck."

• • • •

Bert got his mustang and his gear out of the company stable and was packed and prepared to leave the city shortly before five o'clock. Then James B. Hume showed up. At first sight of him Bert was unable to decipher his expression. If he was angry, it wasn't in his face. He was probably holding it in check deep in his gut, he thought. Hume came striding up to him.

"You damn fool!"

Angry enough, Bert decided.

"James, I'm sorry 'bout what happened out there. I hope Mr. Wolf in snake's clothin' didn't come down on ya too hard."

"He didn't come down on me at all."

"Came down on me out there."

"I wonder why. Of all the idiotic, farfetched, ridiculous buffoonery you've ever pulled, that funeral takes the prize."

"It worked. He showed up."

"Who cares? I don't. Wells Fargo doesn't—"

"I do."

"Listen to me. Before you go off half cocked. Again. I've talked to Tevis. I've done my level best to mollify him. I've been closeted with him for the past four hours. Don't speak, let me finish; I've finally gotten him to reconsider firing you, mostly because of Ben, you understand. Firing Ben, with him practically at death's door, was fairly heavy-handed. Tevis recognizes that. He also sees that he can't keep one of you on and fire the other. So once again, fortunately for us all, he's willing to forgive and forget. It wasn't easy. Just one thing, and I know now that you've calmed down, you'll see the fairness of it. He does insist that you apologize. I've assured him you're man enough to. I know you will. He's entitled to that much."

Bert listened with his head down, tugging at his latigo straps, ruffling the horse's mane, checking straps here and there.

"So you can forget what happened," continued Hume. "As of an hour ago, you've been reinstated. Apologize and we'll just pick up and go on from here."

"You pick up and go on. I'm leavin'."

"You haven't heard a word I've said!" Hume paused, sniffed, and made a disagreeable face. "It stinks in here. Can we continue this outside?"

"Nothin' to continue, and I have, too, heard a word you've said, heard every one. I can't 'pologize for nothin', not to him, on account I don't see anythin' I should 'pologize for. If there's 'pologizin' got to be done, he's the one should be doin' it, not this old boy...."

"You both lost your tempers!"

"I didn' lose nothin'."

"Egbert..."

"James, I know ya mean well. If there's 'pologizin' deserved, it's from me to you. I do 'pologize from the heart for embarrassin' ya, and for the hoodwinkin', but you can understand how I had to do it, had to—what ya call—resort to desp'rate measures, and it worked. You saw. If that flea-bitten nag hadn't'a thrown me I'd'a chased him and caught him before Daly City and he'd be lyin' on a slab at Widenhall and Smithers this very minute. So I 'pologize and I quit, which ya already know I have."

He offered his hand to shake. Hume glowered at it. He was suddenly making fists and trembling, his jowls quivering, his face reddening, threatening to purple.

"You obstinate old coot!"

"Old? I'm forty-three, you're past fifty. Who ya callin' old?"

"You're incorrigible! All right, quit, I wash my hands of you! Go on, beat it!"

"I'm goin'," said Bert calmly. He mounted. "Ya gonna say good-bye pleasant and wish me luck, or we gonna part like this, with you standin' there shakin' like a bowl o' jelly fit to split your seams and bust open your ulcer? We partin' friends or no?"

"Get... out... of... here!"

"Good-bye, see ya 'round."

Five

Over the course of the next four weeks Bert drifted southward, zigzagging down to near the border, surviving on bits and scraps of information, their sum fashioning a mosaic of movement on the part of Rance Cutler that appeared both logical and pursuable. Cutler made one strategic mistake that Bert was quick to seize on. Were he in the outlaw's boots and found himself short of cash, he would have pulled off only one job in order to secure all the money he would need for the trek. But Cutler struck four times before he got to the border. Bert knew him to be a spendthrift, and it was just possible that as soon as he got his hands on a sum, he frittered it away, rendering it necessary to go right back to work. But four holdups in four weeks, and the publicity they generated, made it easy to follow him.

Too easy? wondered Bert as he came within sight of the border. Could it be that Cutler wanted to make certain he'd be followed, wanted him to eventually catch up with him so they could have it out once and for all? He wouldn't put it past him.

It had been a rugged nearly nine hundred miles; sleep failed to restore Bert's bones and muscles; decent food did not rekindle his energy as it usually did. His horse, too, was tired. What she needed was to be turned loose in a field of grama for two weeks with plenty of fresh water available. With this in mind he stopped at a cattle ranch near Gadsden on the Colorado River and swapped her for a fresh mount, a tough Indian pony, white and bay with the devil in her eye, a breed blessed with unusual endurance and strength, necessary assets for the trek ahead.

The latest information to come Bert's way were a few lines near the end of an item in the *Brawley Gazette*, a rehash of the few facts known about Cutler's successful robbery of the Salton bank six days earlier. The culprits had gotten away, of course, but all four had later been seen riding toward the border. The following morning Lady Luck smiled her warmest in weeks on Bert. A posse from Salton had pursued Cutler and his henchmen a mile into Mexico. There had been a shoot-out. Cutler, carrying the loot, had gotten away unscathed; two of his three men were killed, the third was wounded slightly and brought back to Salton. Suddenly finding himself facing the gallows, he unburdened his conscience, cooperating admirably with the men who questioned him. He described in detail the one-eyed one's exploits since Dixon up north in Solano country, scene of his first and only lone-hand holdup after fleeing San Francisco. Most helpful to Bert was the disclosure that Cutler was heading for Durango, deep in the heart of the Mexican state of the same name. Durango's attraction, according to the informant, was a woman.

It all hung together for Bert. Upon learning of it, on subsequent second thought did it make sense because he wanted it to so badly? Was the man telling the truth or deliberately misleading his listeners, knowing he'd be quoted in the papers? Were Durango and the woman who waited a carefully prepared fabrication? It wouldn't be the first time

Cutler had thrown misinformation his way. But true or false, it was all Bert had to go on.

Durango threatened a discouragingly long haul, what could very possibly turn out to be a nearly twelve-hundred-mile wild-goose chase. About half the distance, all the way to Ciudad Obregon, he could travel the Sonoran Desert country, avoiding the Sierra Madre Occidental. The thought did little to cheer him; it was like choosing between being bitten by a wolf or clawed by a cougar. Still, mountain travel would slow him to a fraction of his daily pace down the desert. Actually he could get as far down as the port of Mazatlán. From there he could cut sharply northeast and cross the mountains to Durango.

As harsh as desert travel was this time of year—early August—at least the Sonoran sands would not be overrun with roving bands of *bandidos*, as were the mountains. Only rattlesnakes, scorpions, and *garrapata*, a particularly tenacious tick of the northern deserts. Scorpions were everywhere there was sand, but the scorpion capital of North America had to be Durango. So plentiful were they there, craftsmen imbedded them in glass and sold the products as jewelry and ashtrays. But the scorpion's sting was agonizingly painful and sometimes fatal.

By sand or soaring heights it would take him close to eight weeks to reach his destination, even if the weather held favorably. But the more he thought about it, the more he itched to tackle it. Deep in his heart he acknowledged that even if Cutler rode all the way to Patagonia until he ran out of dry land, Bert would follow him. He would have to. It was not now, nor had it ever been, a matter of choice.

Thinking about Cutler brought thoughts of Bert's wife, Ariel; he pictured the stagecoach stopped by Cutler and his men, the passengers ordered out and lined up in the road to be relieved of their money and valuables. Cutler ordered everyone to turn out his pockets. Ariel had reached into her bag. Cutler was sitting on his horse not fifteen feet from her. He'd shot twice. Both bullets had struck her in the chest. She'd died instantly.

He then casually blew the smoke from his gun and

explained his action to the shocked onlookers. She'd been reaching for a derringer, he told them. He had one of his men turn her bag upside down, emptying it. The contents fell into the dust. There was no derringer. She was mortally afraid of guns. He couldn't even get her to hold one. The mere sight of any kind of weapon whitened her cheeks. She was twenty-five at the time of her death. She had been away six weeks visiting her family in eastern Kansas. She was due to arrive home in Stockton on Ben's birthday, his seventh. The party was waiting for her.

Father and son's paths had crossed Cutler's no fewer than five times since that tragic day fifteen years ago. Every time they got him on the hook, he managed to wriggle off or was helped off by friends or an uncooperative fate. But the day of final reckoning was coming, even if it—like Durango—was twelve hundred miles away.

"If it's twelve thousan', I'm comin', ya scum. I got six for ya. You've earned 'em ten times over and you're gonna get 'em."

Beautiful Ariel. The most wonderful thing that had ever happened in his otherwise drab life. Glistening chestnut hair; dark, flashing eyes; and a smile that set his heart glowing at the sight. Such a little slip she was, almost frail-looking. When they were courting, he'd been afraid to hold her in his arms lest he break a bone. He remembered telling her; how she had laughed. Little girl mine. Ariel.

"I love you, only you...."

He stopped in Gadsden long enough to send a wire to Wynn Esterhazy, the Wells Fargo agent in Casper, Wyoming, and an old friend, one of nearly three hundred agents Ben and he had helped out of scrapes over the years. He asked Wynn to telegraph Ben in care of the home office in San Francisco, and that it was to appear that the message was coming from him. Ben was nobody's fool, to be sure; more than likely he'd ignore it, suspecting that it was only a ruse, but maybe, just maybe—in light of the fact that he had nothing else to go on—he might set out for Wyoming when he was able to travel again. Wyoming was as nice this time of year as Idaho, and it would put him out of harm's way by a good sixteen hundred miles.

His telegram dispatched, he mounted, heeled his pony, and rode off south-southwest. Half an hour later he crossed over into Mexico.

● ● ● ●

Ben sat in James B. Hume's office. He was healing fast and well; his ordeal had stripped him of almost eighteen pounds, which he resolved to restore to his frame as speedily as possible. He attributed his recovery to three things.

"First-rate doctor, luck, and Bert."

Hume stumped out his cigar and eyed him questioningly. "Egbert?"

"He gave me blood. It gave me the shove I needed to start me down the road to recovery. It's been four weeks; I wonder where he's gotten to?"

"Not Casper..."

"Not a chance. My guess is Mexico. Only where specifically?"

"Wherever, *vaya con Dios*." Hume smiled. "I honestly hope you don't find out. If you do, you'll go chasing off after him, bother the shape you're in."

"I'm in good shape, nearly a hundred percent."

"Good for you. I'll take your word for it. Ready to go back to work?"

Before Ben could answer, the door opened. As usual, Lloyd Tevis entered without bothering to knock. He greeted Ben with a broad, if artificial, smile; he congratulated him on how well he looked.

"Ready to go back to work, are you?"

"Itching to." Ben cleared his throat. "As soon as Bert gets back."

Tevis's face clouded. He got out an Old Judge and fitted it to his cigarette holder. Hume lit a match for him. He blew smoke at President Grant, staring at him from the wall behind Hume's desk, positioned squarely between portraits of Henry Wells and William Fargo.

"That'll be never," said Tevis icily. "Your father made quite clear his feelings about Wells Fargo. You must know he quit."

"He was just blowing off steam. He'll be back."

Tevis eyed him through smoke. "Would it offend you if I speak frankly?"

"You don't want him back."

"Wouldn't you say the feeling's mutual? I would. Wouldn't you, Jim?"

"I'll talk to him," said Ben.

"Jim already has, isn't that so, Jim? Like a Dutch uncle." Tevis snickered. "Might as well talk to the wind off the bay."

"Let me understand," said Ben. "What you're saying is, even if he agrees to let bygones by bygones, you refuse to take him back."

"It's hardly up to him to agree to let bygones be anything. He alone is responsible for this breach. He started it with that fake funeral. I don't know if you've read the follow-up stories in the newspapers, but he's made Wells Fargo look a laughingstock. Deliberately. I hate to say it, but he's a vengeful man. I can be pushed so far and no farther. I'm sorry. Actually, since we're on the subject, I must say it's you we're interested in: your welfare, your future, not his."

"If you don't want him, you don't want me."

"Ben!" burst Hume.

"I mean it."

"I'm sure you do," said Tevis loftily. "Whatever you say, lad. Now, if that's all, would you mind excusing us? We do have a business to run."

"Gentlemen, gentlemen—"

"Forget it, Jim," snapped Tevis, "he's made it clear how he feels. The least we can do is respect his decision. I believe you have sick-leave money coming to you, Ben. You're also entitled to your severance, of course."

"Good day, gentlemen."

Hume followed Ben to the door, appealing to him to stay.

"Let's just talk it over. What harm can that do? Ben . . ."

"I'm sorry, James. Good-bye."

"Let him go," said Tevis as the door closed. "Good riddance, I say. Let's talk about that depot robbery in Salinas. I'm not altogether satisfied with the reports."

"Stick Salinas in your ear, blast you!"

Hume snatched up his out box and flung it, contents and all, against the wall, narrowly missing President Grant. Tevis snickered.

"Temper, temper. By the way, I almost forgot, you and I had a wager. I offered you two to one that Slaughter would quit. He did. You owe me a dollar."

Six

Ben sat alone in a booth in a restaurant down the block from the Wells Fargo building. In front of him sat a half-filled cup of coffee. His fury had subsided into annoyance, which now seemed to be giving way to worry.

"You've never quit before. I know you've threatened to a hundred times, but you never stepped over the line."

"It couldn't be helped. 'Sides, I didn't step, I was pushed."

"You can come back."

"No thanks. I shoulda quit the day that wolf in snake's clothin' took over. Ya know he plain stole the company right out from under Henry Wells and Bill Fargo's noses."

"He did not." They were both shortsighted—what am I saying?—stone-blind to the inevitability of the railroads. They despised the very idea. They not only declined to invest, they actively discouraged others. Stanford, Huntington, and the rest of the railroad people hardly could be expected to forgive and forget. Tevis pulled a coup; he had the foresight to, and he did it."

"He outeuchered Henry and Bill."

"That's hardly stealing. His Pacific Union Express company had an exclusive contract with the U.P."

"And he forced Wells Fargo to pony up five million bucks for it, holdin' it like a sword over the company's head. If that's not stealin', I'd like to know what you call it!"

"Bert, if that's stealing, two thirds of all multimillion dollar business deals are."

"Who says they're not?"

"What you seem determined to overlook is that Wells Fargo would never have survived if he hadn't taken over. You'd have been out of a job eleven years ago."

"And be grateful today."

"What's the use? Why try to talk sense to you? When will I ever learn?"

"Is everything all right, sir?"

It was the waitress. She smiled down at him somewhat pityingly, he imagined. He could feel his cheeks redden. What else can being caught talking to oneself do but generate embarrassment!

"Fine, ahhh..."

"A little more coffee?"

"Thank you."

She filled his cup, smiled again, and glided off. He sealed his lips to prevent their moving. Where was Bert? What was happening to him? Why was it that everytime he got on Cutler's tail he did so in the heat of anger, the worst possible mental condition in preparation for a showdown! Where would it be this time? Mexico, certainly, but where exactly? It was possible that neither of them knew at this stage. The one-eyed one had a good six hours' head start. He'd no doubt stop to hold up one or two banks on the way down to finance his travels, but with all Bert's stopping, to question people, to buy every newspaper in sight in search of information and clues, it was doubtful he'd catch up with him before Cutler got to where he was going.

"Where?"

He looked up. The waitress was behind the counter, still holding her coffeepot, still smiling at him. He smiled back self-consciously and sipped.

His mind raced back over the years, to college in Virginia. To commencement. Rows and rows of spindle-back chairs filled with parents and siblings and friends. And Bert sitting in the back row, squirming uncomfortably in the June heat. He wore a linen suit purchased especially for the occasion, and sterling celluloid cuffs and collar, inside of which he was constantly running his finger around, to separate it from his skin, afflicted with prickly heat. His boiled shirt was brand-new, carried in its box all the way from California, and his heavy French brocade silk tie a winter tie. When he greeted him at the railroad station, Bert, unwilling to wait until he got to his hotel room, showed him his shirt and tie. Ben hadn't the heart to tell him that it was a winter tie. The one sartorial concession Bert refused to make was a hat. Before starting out, he decided that his Stetson would be out of place, so he left it home and went without a hat.

Sitting up on the stand a little to the right of the speaker's lectern with his fellow graduates, Ben could see Bert in the rear row. He was the only one of more than eighty fathers fingering inside his collar and leaning forward, the better to see everything that was going on up front. The sight of Bert and his unabashed enthusiasm for the occasion did not embarrass him. So proud was Bert that he was practically bursting his buttons. When Ben's name was called and he went up to accept his diploma, he watched Bert out of the corner of his eye. It was *then* that embarrassment struck in all its fury. He could see Bert regaling everybody within earshot, telling one and all, he was sure: "That's my boy, that's Ben, he's summer come louder." (Since then he had never been able to get him to pronounce *summa cum laude* correctly.) Not that it mattered. Only then and there he carried on so that he drew everyone's attention, including Dr. Corbett's, the university president. Two of Bert's neighbors finally managed to calm him down in diplomatic fashion. The ceremony resumed, he was handed his diploma, then Dr. Corbett shook his hand and commented good-naturedly on Bert's "enthusiasm," and that was that.

When the last name was called and the last speaker had his say, everyone rose to sing the national anthem, after which parents, graduates, and faculty swarmed about, introducing each other and chatting. Ben introduced his senior year professors to Bert. Bert had something highly original to say to each one: "Isn't this boy the smartest brain you ever had the pleasure o' teachin' bar none? Summer come louder." Or, "You ever give out higher marks to any pupil in your whole life teachin'?" Or, "I don't know whether Bert's tolja or not, but I never even got outta grade school...."

Lemonade and cookies were served. Bert promptly spilled lemonade down his new shirtfront, narrowly missing Dr. Corbett's, excusing himself and confessing that he "didn't much go for lemonade, anyhow," that bourbon was his speed, that he hadn't had a drink in six days, and now that the whole shebang was over, he was looking forward to curling up with a bottle that night. This he determinedly imparted to Dr. Corbett, unaware that the man was a staunch Baptist and confirmed teetotaler.

Like a heifer wandering through a vegetable garden leaving disaster in its wake, Bert left a trail of faux pas and unintentional sarcasm and insults strewn all over the campus of the University of Virginia. At the time summa cum laude thought in all seriousness he was leaving a legend in his wake. For years later faculty and alumni would recall the man from California with the winter tie and the finger inside his collar.

But Ben did not criticize Bert, not once. He could see how out of place he felt, how self-conscious, but, at the same time, how extraordinarily pleased, overjoyed. It was a different world, and he didn't begin to fit into it. His attire alone and his discomfort inside it made him stand out like a sore thumb.

But he tried—Lord in heaven, he tried—and later, on the train home, Ben, told him how glad he was he'd come, how proud he was of him, how grateful he was to be his son. And meant every syllable.

Good-bye, Charlottesville, books and classes, grades and pranks; hello, Wells Fargo.

"Good-bye, Wells Fargo."

He finished his coffee, left money, and went out, turning his step toward Wells Fargo. He would collect the money due him, then leave town. For where? He hadn't the slightest idea. On second thought, why go running off after a will-o'-the-wisp? Bert's phony telegram had arrived; perhaps, in time, disclosure of his true whereabouts would come.

"That'll be the day."

He caught himself. He really should stop talking to himself. Two women passersby were eyeing him quizzically. Yes, shed the habit by all means.

The only trouble was that without Bert around he *had* nobody to talk to but himself.

• • • •

Bert was suffering the same problem. His conversational partner boasted four legs, however. With laudable endurance and, for him, infinite patience, he made his way down western Mexico to the port of Mazatlán, where he fell into a bit of unexpected luck. He discovered that in El Salto, a stone's throw more than two hundred miles up into the mountains to the northeast, a newly completed rail line began, carrying passengers and freight all the way to Durango.

He departed Mazatlán on his fourth horse, counting the Indian pony acquired at the cattle ranch in Gadsden some six weeks before. Number four was a sturdy-legged mustang, well adapted to the mountainous terrain that lay ahead. Bert looked forward to the mountains; they'd be a relief from the sandy wastes through which he had suffered southward. Two of his horses had suffered even more than he did. Both died of overwork. Each time it happened, he felt conscience-stricken over it; it only served to alert him to the fact that he was so preoccupied with the pursuit that he didn't even consider that the horse under him had no such monomaniacal fixation to prod it forward.

He also fell prey to sunstroke. It was the first time in his life; it embarrassed him. It struck him just before he crossed the Rio Yaqui, having come almost to within sight of Cocorit. It was a blistering day, so hot breath burned in his lungs. Impatient with his interminable sweating, his hatband gluing itself to his brow, he foolishly draped his hat down his back, holding it in place with its leather string around his neck. At first, cautiously mindful of the harshness of the sun, he resolved to ride bareheaded for only a few minutes, but it was such a relief to his well-chafed forehead, he did not restore his hat. He had a full head of hair, he reasoned. "No sun's gonna' knock me out."

Within sight of the river he suddenly keeled over, tumbling unconscious from his saddle. Luck was with him—not only did he not break his neck, but also, within minutes, passersby found him and took him into town to be treated.

He awoke in a hospital bed, his pulse weak and unusually rapid; he was also seeing double. By the next morning the danger had passed and he felt fine. At noon when he was discharged, he didn't need the nurse's stern warning that from now on he keep his hat on. It wasn't the sun that had knocked him out, he told himself, it was the sun combined with his weariness. He knew he was run-down, he felt run-down; when he got to Durango, he would have to take a couple days to get his strength back before tackling Cutler. He had to be sharp for the showdown, mentally as well as physically prepared.

Would he find Cutler in Durango? he asked himself for the hundredth time, riding out of Mazatlán. He would, with luck and with his guard down, though Cutler would be a fool not to expect that he was being followed. No fool he. Was the mysterious woman his only sidekick, or would he come upon him to find him surrounded by a new gang? Time would answer all his questions.

Leaving the Sinaloa-Nayarit coast, he moved into the Piedmont ridges, picking his way gradually higher until he was deep into the Sierra Madre Occidental. The scenery was magnificent climbing eastward. He could see for fifty miles in every direction. It was noticeably and enjoyably cooler. Day after day the skies were bright and immaculately clear. Deer were plentiful, moving fearlessly through the trees, unaccustomed to the sight of man and horse. He saw bear four days in a row and once a pair of big cats. From a distance they looked like jaguars, but he only got a quick glimpse of them before they vanished.

Ten days of riding from dawn until dusk brought him to little, cobblestoned El Salto, built around a huge and badly cracked fountain, its streets and alleyways shared by people and chickens. There, to his chagrin, he was told that the engine that pulled the only train back and forth to Durango had blown its boiler, and the parts necessary to repair it were not expected to arrive for another week to ten days. He rested a day and went on.

On the afternoon of the twentieth day since he had left Mazatlán, rising ahead of him he saw the twin towers of a massive and imposing Tuscan-style structure, splashed by the sun, with shadowed niches at three levels. The cathedral. Durango.

Cutler!

He pulled up to stare at the sight in awe and relief. At last. He began unscrewing the cap of his canteen. He was preparing to drink when he heard sounds left and right behind him: hooves, stones dislodged and rolling, a voice.

"'Ands up and keep 'em there, cully."

Seven

James Hume refused to let Ben sever the tie of friendship between them. He found him a rooming house and visited him after work every day. The two dined together frequently and took long walks on Sundays. Ben's beef was against Lloyd Tevis, not Hume. The latter's finest asset was his great, good heart; as badly as Bert had used him, Hume harbored no resentment.

He had always given Ben the impression that he secretly saw himself as a second father; over the years it had gradually become a relationship that fit somewhere between father and uncle. Hume was by nature easygoing and rarely given to temperamental outbursts, unless prodded by others. Tevis could prod him but few others. Give "Uncle" James his favorite Cuban cigar, his rose garden, his collection of scenic views of San Francisco and the Bay Area, and his stereoscope with its polished cherrywood frame, give him his cat Eloise, his bachelorhood, and a decently cooked meal and he was content. Unlike Tevis, he was no slave to ambition, not a workaholic, not Wells Fargo's prisoner. Unlike Tevis, people liked him.

Ben liked him very much. He'd always been straightforward and fair with him, a true friend. He could be boring and overly picayune. He was the most fastidious dresser Ben had ever known, in marked contrast to his father, who couldn't care in the least what he wore or how it made him look.

Ben told Hume things one only tells a trusted friend and confidant, knowing that they would never get back to the office. As did his father. Subtly but unceasingly, Hume worked on Ben to get him to reconsider quitting the company. His view was that Ben had only done so out of loyalty to Bert, not dislike for Tevis. Father and son had always disliked Tevis; there could hardly be any increase in Ben's antipathy for the man. Hume raised a valid argument for his staying on, noting that if and when Bert contacted Ben, he would undoubtedly need help. Ben could provide it, and Wells Fargo could help. Dozens of detectives on the payroll would willingly lend a hand. Wells Fargo men always stuck together. In unity there was strength, that sort of thing. And Tevis's disapproving voice would be lost in the uproar of indignation.

But perhaps an even stronger argument was the older man's conviction that regardless of Bert's decision and his current resentment toward the company, sooner or later he'd return to the fold. For Bert Slaughter to be out of Wells Fargo was like taking a fish out of water. Ben could not disagree with this. Bert never had considered that he worked for Lloyd Tevis. In his heart of hearts he worked for James B. Hume and for the other two hundred and fifteen detectives, crusaders all, riding about the territories on their white horses, collaring miscreants on black horses, doing their daily best to make the West safe for decent people and Wells Fargo agents, many of whom were one and the same. It wasn't a job, it was a mission; and he could no more renounce it permanently than shave his head and enter a monastery in Tibet. Chase and collar was in his blood and always would be. Lloyd Tevis was president and chief executive officer of nothing, in Bert's scheme of things. He was a sliver in a finger, a petty annoyance, a target to vent his spleen at, Ice-eyes, Mr. Wolf in snake's clothing.

Ben found it hard to disagree with any of Hume's observations. Yes, he acknowledged, out of Hume's hearing, that Bert *would* be back and he with him. *After* Cutler was taken care of. In a way it was good that it had worked out as it had. Quitting the company, Bert was now free to concentrate all his time and energies on the one-eyed one, and punch his ticket once and for all.

If only he'd get in touch!

• • • •

Herbert Howland was a cockney ne'er-do-well originally from Battersea in London. He had been run out of town at an early age, settling in Southampton and run out of there, then stowing away aboard a Boston-bound freighter. Once arrived, he resumed his criminal activities, eventually leaving Boston one step ahead of the police, cheating and stealing his way westward, settling nowhere in particular, laboring by his lonesome, and later in the company of others of his stripe from the Mississippi to the ocean, from Canada to Mexico.

His face resembled a skull over which the skin had been stretched and glued in place. His eyes were deep-set and shifty, his teeth prominent, his ears oversize, the lobes like dewlaps, lending him the look of a clownish death's-head. He had been in America for nearly fifteen years, but his accent marked him as newly arrived. He wore a battered derby hat, a silk vest, and numerous rings, along with the working outfit of a drover. He was partial to Irish whiskey, fish, chips, and bangers, which he had a hard time finding this side of the Atlantic, and women a foot taller than he.

He had recognized Bert on sight and, with his three companions, took him prisoner, riding him off to a mountain cabin about a mile north of the capture site. The place was a pigsty, stinking of stale liquor and body odor. A deer carcass hung from the exposed rafters, and cups and plates stacked by the sink looked as if they hadn't been scraped in weeks.

"Hegbert, Hegbert, Hegbert," cooed Howland, "hit's been bloody hayges. Lads, meet Hegbert Slaughter, a bloomin' toff in the rough, a bloke and a 'alf, salt o' the hearth, and Wells Fargo's foinest copper. 'E nabbed me up in Boulder in Coloradi ten years back and got me a four-year vaykaytion in the penny-tenchary in Canyon City, 'e did. Armed robbery, roight, old china? Tell 'em. . . ."

"You tell 'em, Herb."

"Back then oi was real balmy and a bit on the 'owlin' side, tell 'em, Hegbert."

His three companions looked like highly successful losers, their eyes permanently stamped with fear and worry, little to say, little in their heads but memories of past close shaves with the law, captivities, brief flush periods, and more longer stretches when all the hands were busted flushes, all the meals cold, and life, such as it was, had to be snatched at on the run. All four had to be wanted, thought Bert. What else would they be doing down here?

To give the devil his due, though, Herb Howland was no killer. In his day he likely had killed, but he didn't make a practice of it like Cutler. Still, he had caught him in Boulder with the goods—two mail sacks and a chest full of gold coins, he recalled—testified against him in court, heard him found guilty, and watched him march off to prison. It wasn't a slice of nostalgia to give him warm and friendly feelings.

"Four years in that 'ole was like four years in a bloody packing case, Hegbert." He laughed thinly. "And not once did you come to visit me, old dear. . . ."

"I was gonna one Christmas, but I busted my hip."

Howland laughed uproariously.

"What is all this, Herb, what do ya tie me up and drag me to this hole for? Whattaya want from me?"

"Before we get into that, tell me what you're doing wandering around these 'ills? A bit off the beaten track, wouldn't you say? Couple thousand miles off. Who you chaysing? Gorblimey, don't tell me! Not Ransom Cutler, not old one-peeper, not still? You been after 'im must be twenty years."

"Only fifteen. You haven't seen him have you?"

"He's in Duryngo, tipplin' and lazyin' and throwin' 'is plosh about."

"Untie me, lemme go, I gotta get after him."

"Pytience, pytience, first things first. When we're done wiv you, you can go on your merry wye. You can go into town and blow 'im from 'ere to Eagle Pass for all we care."

"Through with me? Through what?"

"We... Gorblimey, forgive my bad manners. Permit me to introduce my three cullies; meet Cyril, Algernon, and 'orace Pittman, the Pittman brothers, lyte of Fort McKevatt, Texas. Sy 'ello to Hegbert, lads. Hegbert, bryce your bones and 'old on to your 'at, we're 'oldin' you for ransom."

"What!"

"You're Wells Fargo's top copper, number one. You're worth a bloomin' packet to them. They'll pye dearly, willingly, and cheerfully to get you back sayfe and sound. What do you say to ten thousand?"

Bert snorted. "You're crazy with the heat. Old Ice-eyes wouldn't pay ten cents for me. Won't give ya a red cent, seein' as I'm no longer with the company. I quit two months ago."

"Wot a perishin' liar you are, shayme on you!"

"It's the bald truth! I quit."

Howland bent over and, rummaging through his pockets, fished out Bert's wallet.

"Wot we got 'ere? Your bloomin' ID card says you're still on the job."

"I forgot to throw it away. You do it for me, tear it up."

"Not on your life, this little card's our ticket. 'Ere, Cyril, tayke it. You lads ride into town and send off a tellygram. To Wells Fargo in San Francisco. Tell 'em who we got, say wot's on the card to prove it, see you get 'is number in there, they'll recognize it, and tell 'em we want ten thousand and in seven dyes, or we'll send 'is 'ands back in a bloomin' greaser mail pouch. 'Op to it!"

• • • •

James B. Hume's perspiration set his pink face glistening. John J. Valentine, company superintendent, looked similarly anxious; only Lloyd Tevis appeared undisturbed. A picture of serenity, he puffed on his cigarette and eyed the gossamer smoke.

"Ten thousand," he said quietly, "quite a sizable sum, gentlemen."

Valentine, a flinty-eyed, bull-chested man in his late fifties, was a hard-bitten veteran of the company's early wars of competition. His praiseworthy record, combined with his devotion to candor, encouraged him to speak bluntly, whoever his listener.

"You're talking about a man's life," he said evenly, then looked to Hume as if to demand his support silently.

"John's right, sir," said Hume obligingly.

"Are we really? Do you think that riffraff would actually murder him if we didn't pay? I'm not saying we're not going to. Still..."

"Yes?" both asked.

"What would it accomplish? Oh, they'd probably let him go; there is that kind of honor among thieves, but realistically, what do you expect would happen?"

"What?" asked Hume.

"I'd expect that half the outlaws in the country, certainly plenty of those who prey on us, would attempt the same monkeyshines. We could end up with scores of agents kidnapped, held for ransom. We could go broke in six months."

Hume shrugged and fastened his eyes on Valentine in a manner that suggested he was determined not to look at the speaker.

"We could. That settles it. We ignore this wire and wait for Egbert's hands to show up in the mail. I don't imagine they'll forward his entire corpse, not all the way from Mexico."

Tevis was glaring at him. "I don't see the point of making a joke of it."

Death In Durango

"And I don't see the point of even discussing it. An employee's life is in jeopardy."

"Former employee," corrected Tevis.

"Do we meet their demands or don't we?" asked Valentine. "What do you say, John?"

"I say send the money."

Tevis smiled frigidly, sighed, and shook his head. He suddenly looked a martyr. "I must be doing something all wrong...."

Hume looked up. "Beg your pardon?"

"You two always seem to side against me. I'm always outvoted. All right, all right, all right, but I still say we're making a mistake. We'll be setting a bad precedent."

There was a knock. Albertina Preble, Hume's pretty blonde secretary, stuck her head in.

"Excuse me, gentlemen. Mr. Hume, Mr. Slaughter is here to see you."

"What the devil!" burst Tevis. He glared at Hume.

"I sent word over to his boardinghouse as soon as I finished reading the wire," said Hume. "You don't for a minute imagine I'd hold something like this back from him, do you?"

"Not for a minute," said Valentine evenly.

Ben showed up behind Miss Preble.

"Come in, come in," sang Tevis loftily.

He got up and placed a chair for Ben. Hume handed him the telegram.

"My God..."

"Don't worry, lad," said Tevis, "the money's as good as on its way. Will be in five minutes. We certainly can't leave a loyal employee dangling in the wind."

"Ten thousand..."

"The amount's really not the issue," Tevis went on. "Getting him back safe and sound is all that counts."

"This came from Durango," said Ben.

His eyes had yet to abandon the paper in his hand. He suddenly jumped to his feet and started for the door.

"Where are you going?" asked Hume.

"Where do you think?" He paused, his hand on the side

of the door. "Thank you, Mr. Tevis, I appreciate it. Thank you, James, Mr. Valentine. I won't forget this. I owe Wells Fargo; we both do."

"Wait, wait..." called Hume.

But he has gone.

● ● ● ●

Accompanied by the Pittman brothers, Herbert Howland was en route to Nombre de Dios on the Mezquital River, southeast of Durango. He had visited there alone two days before to get, as he put it, "the lie of the setup." Nombre de Dios was quite like a hundred other towns studding the heights of central Mexico: picturesque with its shops and stalls and whitewashed church; neglected; and thanks to the coolness of the air at sixty-four hundred feet, slightly more bustling than other lowland towns. It boasted one distinction that set it apart from the surrounding mountain towns, however. Its bank held nearly seventy percent of all the silver mined in the area.

Howland had a fondness for silver. Both the silver and the need to elude the law north of the border for an extended period were what had brought him to Mexico. Gold was all right, money excellent, jewelry he did not disdain, but his favorite valuable was silver. In any form. The quote from the poem "The Lost Leader"—"just for a handful of silver he left us" would have suited him. For such a quantity he would denounce his best friend or abandon his only child, had he a child to leave.

It was a magnificent day: the mountains glowed in the late-afternoon sunlight; the comfortable air was clear and sweet to the taste; a lone *zopilote,* a turkey buzzard, floated high on a thermal draft, asleep on the wing from all appearances; and the silver waited less than five miles away. At the rear of the little caravan Horace Pittman sat at the reins on a small donkey cart. All four wore serapes and wide-brimmed straw hats and had darkened their faces and hands with stain. All four were armed with pistols and rifles, the latter concealed in cloths.

"You think Wells Fargo'll send the money?" asked Cyril, riding behind Howland in the lead along the narrow trail.

"It's as good as 'ere. Matter o' fact, oi intend to check out the tellygraph office in Duryngo on the wye back. Wiv it and wot we collect from this afternoon's job we'll be sitting pretty as ducks in a row."

"Do we turn him loose after we gets the money?"

"You think we should, lad?"

"He'll run back to them and . . . and . . ."

"Peach on us, oi been thinking the syme meself. It moight be best if we collect the rino and just pull out. Not go back to the cabin at all."

"He's tied," said Algernon. "He'll starve to death."

"Not if 'e wriggles free. 'E's bloody clever, e'll work hit hout."

"How come you're so nice to him?" asked Cyril. "If I caught up with somebody who put me behind bars for four years, I'd blow 'em apart."

"That's where we differ, you and oi, Cyril. You're lacking in sporting blood, you are. Oi was doing my job, 'e was only doing 'is, and in doing 'is, 'e caught me doing moine. Oi respects 'im for that, old dear. Hits called professionalism, which 'as no plyce for petty grudges and spitefulness."

"You won't shoot him, but you'll let him starve," piped Horace from the rear.

Howland did not respond. Instead he began going over the plan.

● ● ● ●

Bert had been skillfully tied, hands bound to his ankles and behind his back. He was left sitting on the floor almost directly under the hanging deer carcass, which was beginning to add its distinctive odor to the sundry other stenches filling the cabin. He had been trying for two solid hours to loosen his left hand, but the more he pulled, the tighter the rope seemed to become. For a time he imagined it was shrinking, although it was perfectly dry. He was lucky; had it been rawhide, his sweat would be shrinking it.

Herbert Howland was out of his mind, he decided. Tevis would never authorize payment of the ransom he was demanding. Hume would try to talk him into it—so would John Valentine and so would Ben, for that matter—but Tevis wouldn't budge. For any other employee he might; he was many things, but he was not stingy. Unfortunately they despised one another. They couldn't be in the same room together for two minutes without raising their voices.

"Oil and water, that's us, friggin' wolf in snake's clothin' . . ."

Seven days, Howland had said; three had already passed. He was hungry. They had fed him breakfast, cold beans and Jamoka, before tying him, but that was close to seven hours ago. It occurred to him that they might be gone for good, but he couldn't believe that Howland would leave and let him starve to death. He hoped they'd come back from the job fairly sober and postpone celebrating long enough to loosen his bonds and feed him.

Yes, tomorrow would be the fourth day, and it did stink to high heaven in here. Somebody ought to divert the waters of the Mezquital, send them through the place, flush out the stink, wash away the damn deer.

More annoying than the aroma and his bonds was the awareness that Cutler was sitting in Durango with the companion of his ease, relaxing, enjoying life, free, healthy, spared pain and discomfort. God forbid he pack up and leave before he could get out of this mess of spiders and catch up with him.

His glance drifted to the door. It was fashioned of five upright planks joined by two crossboards. A piece the size and roughly the shape of a Green River knife blade was missing from the base of the second plank from the left. He could see the weeds outside, the breeze stirring them. Something was emerging. . . .

A white scorpion. It noticed the opening and made straight for it.

"Of course."

In it came, scratching its way toward him. It was a female; she was carrying her young on her back and the forward part of her tail, tiny white replicas of her. They looked as if they were carved of milk glass. She continued her approach. He sucked in his breath and held it. Bert knew from experience that the sting of a scorpion was very painful. The sting of the Durango white scorpion, however, was often fatal.

She had stopped. She raised her tail, tumbling two of her young from it. They came to life and scrambled soundlessly. Her tail curved upward. She seemed to be flaunting the bulb at the end of it, which contained her poison, secreted in glands. Now the rest of her brood was beginning to desert her back. He counted seven in all. They looked to be old enough to fend for themselves, but their stingers were not yet developed.

He had only their mother to worry about. She still had not moved, other than to lift and quietly wave her tail. She was threatening him; he was sure of it. She started forward. She was about two feet from him when he filled his chest with air a second time, grit his teeth, growled, and dropped as swiftly and as hard as he could on his side, his left shoulder hammering the floor, his upper arm crushing her, her body cracking like a nutshell.

• • • •

Using all four sticks of dynamite he had brought along for the purpose, Herbert Howland blew a hole big enough to drive the donkey cart through in the rear of the bank. The cart, however, remained hidden in the trees some fifty yards back. Inside the bank, Cyril and Howland began shooting wildly as Algernon and Horace set about lugging the silver ingots back to the cart. The job was completed in less than six minutes, only four trips by each man being necessary to relieve the vault of every ingot. The hand truck they found inside was a help. Horace drove the cart away into the mountains to a well-hidden cave that Howland had found the week before. He and the others battled four local *policia* joined by half a dozen outraged, civic-minded residents to a standstill, giving Horace nearly twenty minutes to get clear before they themselves fled.

Howland galloped away, leading his henchmen and laughing uproariously.

"Easy as toikin' sweets from a byby, oi luv it! 'Ar, 'ar, 'ar, 'ar, 'ar!"

He continued laughing, joining by the others, for nearly two miles, before coming upon a sight that abruptly stilled him. Ahead of them sat the cart with Horace perched on the driver's seat, his hands raised as high as he could reach, his face flooded with fear. Howland's heart plunged as he counted eleven *bandidos* surrounding his silver. He, Cyril, and Algernon saw them; they saw him and the battle was on. Before he hit the ground, both guns blazing, he recognized the outlaws' leader.

"Suarez, gorblimey! 'Ey! You sloimy rat! Dirty scum! Get out of 'ere! 'Op hit!"

"Herbeert cheeps and feesh, what you theenk you're doing, robbing my bank? I feex you good! I keel you! Adios!"

Howland responded by blowing his hat off, sending him into a fit of rage. Suarez carried a single six-gun; he quickly emptied it, threw himself down behind the cart, and reloaded. Some of his men had rifles, and all could shoot, as Algernon discovered. Rising on one elbow, the better to aim, he took a slug dead-center in his forehead, reacted in astonishment, moaned lightly, and keeled over dead. Seeing his brother hit, Cyril only grunted, but Horace, still sitting on the driver's seat with his hands raised, exploded. He jumped down on the man nearest him and was wrestling him about, going for his gun when Suarez finished reloading and put a single shot between his shoulder blades.

Two minutes and considerable lead later, Cyril was shot through the heart by two men at the same time. He fell, looking in Howland's direction questioningly, as if asking, "How did we get into this?" Howland found himself alone, outgunned eleven to one. Only one *farajido* had been wounded, and only slightly, a bullet from Howland's gun grazing his shooting hand.

Howland concentrated on Suarez, ignoring the others, who were centering their fire on him. He emptied both his guns and paused, lifting his head slightly, peering about, taking stock. The rock shielding him rose barely ten inches from the ground, and he had no cover to either side.

"You don't stand a bloody chance in 'ell, 'erbert, me boy. Toime to pack hit hin. Porfirio!"

"*Si*, Herbeert. You want to give up. *Bueno. Astuto, amigo*. Drop them and stand up weeth your hands high. *Pronto!*"

Howland complied. His hands were high, but his knees had not yet straightened completely when nine-guns exploded as one. Nine bullets entered his chest; five hurtled into his heart.

"Gorblimey, Oi don't believe it. . . ."

Suarez flew into a rage. "*Madre de Dios! Loco bastardos! Idiotas! Imbeciles!*"

• • • •

Bert estimated that Mother Scorpion had been dead about an hour. Her offspring didn't seem to care. They had scattered about the cabin looking for food. They paid no attention to him. He had long since given up trying to loosen his wrists. He was famished and very thirsty. He fancied that he could down a full bucket of water without stopping, so parched was he. He eyed the pump at the end of the sink. A single drop of water glistened on the lip of the pitcher spout. He licked his lips and, digging his heels in, pushed himself across the floor to the wall. He tried to push himself back up the wall, but with his ankles bound together he was unable to get the necessary leverage. He finally gave it up.

He sat staring at the crushed scorpion. One of her babies had returned and was inspecting her. Was he crying? wondered Bert. *Did* scorpions cry when their hearts were broken? Did scorpions have hearts? The baby looked too tiny to have anything other than eight legs, two claws, a tail, and an appetite.

He heard horses. A number of riders were approaching, many more than four, perhaps ten, even fifteen. His heart surged. Rescue? Up they came. The door flew open. Mexicans, *bandidos*, wearing the traditional crossed bandoliers. A fat-faced, jug-eared man with a drooping mustache leered toothlessly and stomped forward.

"What we got here? All tied up—"

"Undo me! Quick, my wrists feel like they're busted; ankles too. I been like this two whole days, closer to three. It's 'cruciatin'. Quick!"

He was untied. He sat rubbing his wrists and ankles.

"Man, that feels good. I 'preciate this more'n you'll ever know, Señor..."

"Suarez. Porfirio Esteban Luis Danzos Alvaro Manuel Gustavo César Romulo Suarez."

"Bert Slaughter."

"You are *compadre* of Herbeert's, *si?*"

"Not on your tintype. Him and me are blood enemies. Why you think I was all tied up here?"

"You have *argumento*, fight?"

"No fight, he captured me."

"*Como?*"

"He's holdin' me for ransom."

"Ha ha ha!"

"What's so funny?"

"Hold you for ransom? What could he get for you, a sick burro? What?" He crouched beside him. The look of amusement fled his expression. He looked hard, ugly. "You lie, *gringo*."

"I'm not, he—" Bert caught himself. What was he doing? What would this fella do but pick up the ball where Howland had dropped it, no doubt tie him back up, hang on to him, and wait for the money.

"Where is Herbert"

Suarez leered and slit his throat with his thumb. "All four dead. Only you left. To tell me where the rest of the seelver is."

"What silver?" Suarez slapped Bert so hard, he knocked him over. "What the—"

"You don't play games with me, *gringo*. I ask you question, you answer. Where does he hide his seelver? I give you ten seconds to answer." He pulled his gun, set the muzzle against Bert's forehead, and cocked the trigger. "One—"

"Wait, wait, wait, I'm tellin' ya the bald truth. I was his pris'ner. You come barrelin' in here, ya find me tied. Why would he tell me his secrets, then tie me up?"

"You were his *compadre*, his *amigo*. You had what you call a falling out, eh? He got mad, tie you up—"

"That's baloney!"

"To keep you here till he finish robbing the bank in Nombre de Dios, then come back here to kill you. Where is his silver? He has a mountain of it."

"I don't know anythin' 'bout any silver."

"You lie, you know, you Yanquis steek together like glue." He pushed the muzzle harder against his head. "One . . . two—"

"Okay, okay! I'll tell ya. It's buried. That's right, he buried it."

"Where?"

"I dunno."

Suarez had taken down his gun; it came up again sharply.

"Wait, wait, whattaya so itchy trigger-fingered for? Can'tcha even wait for me to finish a sentence? He's the only one knows where it's buried, cross my heart, hope to die. He didn't tell another livin' soul. The thing is, there's a map. He carries it on him. He drew it, he's the only one's ever seen it."

"A map to the seelver."

"Right. He's been down here what, six, seven months? He and those Pittmans musta knocked over at least six banks."

"Seven."

"Whatever, they been pilin' up silver to beat the band. Dozens o' ingots, religious stuff, pitchers, cups, lamps, silverware, everything."

"We know, we been keeping an eye on him, waiting for the beeg haul. Today's. Then we pounce. Now." Suarez stood up and stretched. "Get up. We go back to where we ran into them. He carries the map in his pocket, *si*?"

"No, no, he's got a special hidin' place in the heel o' his boot. Hey, ya got anythin' to eat on ya?"

"Eat later, now we go back."

"I'm starvin'."

"On your feet."

"Whattaya need me for? I told ya everythin' ya gotta know, everythin' I know...."

"We need you to keep us company, and to see if you are telling the truth."

"Why would I lie?"

"To save your skeen."

Bert tried his best to react with suitable outrage. Suarez laughed in his face. Bert's heart raced out of control. They would take him back with them; they would look in Howland's boot heel. At least, they'd try to. When it wouldn't come off, when it didn't prove to be hollow, then what? *Oh, those are different boots. I remember now, just before they left for the job, he changed boots. Claimed the old ones were bustin' down, beginnin' to hurt his feet.*

Sure, he'd deliberately leave behind the boots with the map, sure.

Slaughter, the fat's in the fire for sure, and you're the one stuck it there. Good job. Good luck.

Eight

The *Pacific Queen* was perhaps the most unregal oceangoing vessel Ben had ever seen. From stem to stern she displayed a hundred and twenty feet of rust-coated and peeling steel plate. Rats found permanent residence aboard her, he was sure. Her engines were ancient and sadly abused, and her crew looked to be the leavings of the riffraff that loitered about every port of size, men turned down by choosier masters. Foul-smelling black smoke issued from her single funnel, raising a vast quantity of soot that hailed down upon the deck as she struggled to develop steam. The smoke warded off any venturesome and curious seabirds. She carried twenty-four passengers and a full cargo of timber from Portland, Oregon, down to Panama with numerous stopovers between.

Apart from her disreputable appearance, her age, and countless minor infirmities, Ben found himself seriously wondering if she could remain afloat as far as Mazatlán. If she stayed within sight of shore, at least he could swim for it if she went down. But beggars could not be choosers. She was the first southbound vessel to depart San Francisco, and he counted himself lucky to be able to book passage aboard her on such short notice. James Hume had come down to see him off. They stood on the dock surveying the *Queen*, Hume shaking his head and displaying an expression of disapproval.

"You sure you don't want to wait a day or so, Ben? What difference can a few more hours make?"

"You know the answer to that. I don't mind roughing it as far as Mazatlán. It'll only be five days. It'd take five weeks or more on horseback."

Hume continued to survey the packet. The downpour of soot appeared to be abating.

"She looks like she stinks to high heaven," he said bluntly. "I'd be careful what I eat en route if I were you."

"I intend to."

Ben smiled to himself. It was like being seen off by a doting mother. He extended his hand. Hume shook it.

"I wish I could send twenty men with you, but you know his nibs."

"I've no right to expect help from the company in this. Besides, I don't work for you anymore, remember?"

"We'll rectify that oversight when the two of you get back here safe and sound."

"I appreciate your optimism, but as far as going back to work..."

"Let's not get into that." Ben detected a slight catch in Hume's voice, and his eyes were glistening. "You're not a hundred percent yet, keep that in mind. Take care of yourself, Ben. I hope with all my heart that you catch up with him before he runs into more than he can handle. I trust the long trek down there has given him time to give sober thought to this ridiculous business, and when he gets there, if he does find Cutler, he won't go off half cocked. You, either." He paused and laid a paternal hand on his shoulder. "Promise me you'll keep in touch."

"I will."

A woman passed by them and started up the gangplank.

She was wearing a black velvet mantilla trimmed with lace and matching cloak and carrying a parasol over her shoulder. On her head was a bonnet of white velvet with white blond lace. She smiled at them in passing. She was young and quite beautiful, with dark, flashing eyes, an impertinent nose, and sensuous lips. She had about her a definite air of self-possession. Traveling alone, as she appeared to be, she was no doubt well able to take care of herself. Her complexion, noted Ben, was almost as pale as her bonnet, but the pleasantly cool sea air raised a pinkness in her cheeks. Hume looked after her with undisguised admiration.

"Pleasant conversation should help relieve your boredom."

"Hopefully."

• • • •

Her name was Bridget O'Rourke; her father was Irish, as was her husband; her mother Mexican and "descended from Castillian nobility." She was a widow, Señor O'Rourke having died of influenza the previous winter; at the time of his demise they had been married only seventeen months. She lived in Durango where her husband had been regent of the National Institute. He had been twenty years older than she. She was coming from Portland where she had been visiting her husband's sister.

Two days out of San Francisco approaching Point Concepción (just north of Santa Barbara and nearing Long Beach where there would be a two-hour layover), Ben and she stood at the bow railing, looking out over the tranquil blue sea, both of them talking animatedly.

"That's a coincidence," he said, "I'm on my way to Durango myself. Down to Mazatlán, then overland."

"You're not serious...."

"It appears to be the most direct route."

"The most direct, perhaps, but not the fastest. Did you know it's more than three hundred miles from Mazatlán to Durango? There's no train until you get to El Salto. You'll have to ride horseback, and there is no stage."

"I know, I planned to buy a horse."

"It's about two hundred miles to El Salto. The road is wretched."

"How were you planning to get there?"

"By train, of course."

"But there is no train until—"

"Not from Mazatlán, from Tijuana. The stage runs from San Diego to Tijuana. From there I board the train to Mexacali. It goes down to Hermosillo, to Guaymas, to San Blas, just north of Topolobampo. There you change over to the Chihuahua line, which takes you up to Chihuahua, then south to Torreón and west to Durango. It's roundabout and there is the six-hour layover in San Blas, but it only takes a little more than two days. By packet to San Diego and train to Durango it's less than five days in all. You'd be at least five days on horseback getting from Mazatlán to El Salto." She smiled disarmingly. "Let me be your guide, I shall take you all the way to Durango. The train seats may be hard, but they're not as bad as a saddle. What brings you to Durango?"

"Business."

"What is your business?"

"I'm in banking."

"Are you really? Juan Francisco Ruiz, the president of the Banco de Mexico, was my late husband's best friend. I often dine with him and his lovely wife, Maria. You must let me introduce you."

"Thank you, I'd appreciate it."

"Oh, this is wonderful, and here, when I got aboard in Portland, I said to myself, 'Another long, boring jaunt home.' When I come north, I usually stay at least six weeks since it's such a long distance. But you'll enjoy the train. The scenery is magnificent. I never tire of it."

• • • •

Bert was rapidly tiring of his captivity. Suarez and his men surrounded him on the way to the clearing where the massacre had taken place less than an hour before.

"Not far now," Suarez assured him. "About half a mile."

"*Jefe!*" bawled the man riding just ahead of them.

The point man had come barreling back. "*Soldados!*"

"Pull up! Pull up!" barked Suarez.

Bert grinned at him in spite of the worry that had taken firm root in his heart.

"What's the matter, you and the soldier boys on the outs? *Enemigos?*"

"It is better to be safe, eh? Your Spanish is rotten, stick to *Yanqui*. I speak it *perfecto*, eh? I learned it at my sainted mother's knee. Bless her heart, she taught me everyteeng; made me what I am today. A saint, that's what she was. My father was a peeg, a common thief, *el perro del hortelano*. You understand dog in the manger? My mother was Maria Magdalene in the manger, a saint. I worshiped her."

His eyes were filling with tears. Bert's stomach growled hungrily. The men had gathered around while they waited for the soldiers to pass. They stared at Suarez, their expressions uniformly serious. It was all Bert could do to keep from laughing out loud.

"She was a genius, my sainted mother, a geefted artist, a female Leonardo. She could take a gold or silver coin, melt it down, and, with others like eet, fashioned a beautiful trinket, a piece of jewelry, a cup...."

You stole it and she melted it down and worked it up.

"My father was caught stealing a peeg; thy hanged him. Can you imagine, hanging a man for stealing a stinking peeg? A lousy, swill-eating peeg! Dog in the manger, that was heem. He used to beat me with a steek. You should see the scars on my back, my arms. My mother saved me from his drunken wrath. She was a saint. All the neighbors used to say, 'There goes Saint Teresa.' She saw meestical visions just like St. Teresa. The cross of her rosary was snatched from her hand one day in the street, and when she got eet back, eet was changed into jewels more brilliant than diamonds. Of course, only she could see them. Did you know the same teeng happened to St. Teresa de Cepeda, the Spanish nun Mama was named for? And like St. Teresa, my sainted mother often had a terrible pain in her side; an angel came to her with a lance teeped with fire, which he stuck into her heart."

Bert grunted. Suarez bristled. "You don't believe me!"

"I do, I do!"

"The *soldados* have passed, Chief," said the point man. "We can go on."

They resumed riding.

"How come you know Herbeert?" Suarez asked. "From where?"

"Colorado. We robbed Wells Fargo together."

"He was good, *astuto*, slick, and lucky. A man needs luck in this beesiness. My men and I have been watching heem collect seelver for many months. We are not stupid, we let heem do the work, run the risk, and when he's collected a pile, we take it from heem. You should have seen, I got very angry with these boys for killing heem. How are we to find his loot if we shoot heem and shut his mouth forever, eh? Lucky we came back and found you."

Bert closed his eyes and held his breath as they approached the clearing. Howland's corpse would be wearing the wrong boots; as weak a tale as it was, it was all he could think of. He never could think on an empty stomach, let alone with a gun at his head, which Suarez's had been and practically still was.

"*Caramba!*" he snarled.

"Nobody here, *Jefe*," bawled the man beside him.

"I can see, you eediot! The police who chased them from Nombre de Dios caught up and took back their bodies. *Bastardos!*"

"Maybe they buried them here...."

"You don't see any signs of digging, do you? No, interfering peegs took them back to town. If I'd only known about his heel..."

Bert did his level best to conceal his sign of relief but failed to completely. Suarez glared at him.

"What are you theenking, eh? What is running through your mind?"

"I'm hungry! I keep tellin' ya..."

"You'll eat after we get the map."

"How ya gonna get it now?"

"How do you suppose? We'll go into town, just you and me in disguise, eh? Go to the morgue; I'll theenk up some story so we can get in to see Herbeert's body. Before the undertaker undresses heem. Come, we ride to our *escondrijo*. Ha! I have it! We will disguise ourselves as *soldados*. I will be a captain and you my *ayudanta de campos*. Perfect! Brilliant!"

"Except for one thing," said Bert, "where ya gonna get the uniforms?"

"Ha, you would be surprised what we have back at the *escondrijo*."

"It's a crazy idea."

"Nothing of the kind. Army officers can get in anywhere, do most anything; nobody asks questions. They are above the law and the ceevilian population. It is a stupendous idea. *Genio*! I have my sainted mother to thank for my many inspirations of the brain. I owe my brilliance to her. I could have been another Juarez. I am a master strategist, tactician. Ask any of my men, they'll tell you. I command loyalty and respect like the most revered general. Like Caesar! Like Presidente Sebastian Lerdo de Tejada. Did I tell you my sainted mother once read *el presidente*'s palm? Eet was before he was elected, when he was head of the Supreme Court, but she did. She told heem that one day he would be forced to banish Porfirio Diaz, who she named me for. She told de Tejada he would have to, and eet came to pass."

"Good."

"What do you mean, 'good'? You don't believe me?"

"I believe ya, I believe ya! How come ya always think I don't believe ya?"

"Enough talk, time is wasting. You and I must get disguised and get to Nombre de Dios before it is too late, before somebody steals Herbeert's boots, eh? Those undertakers are born thieves. They stole the gold out of my father's tooth when they were getting heem ready for his coffin."

Bert was no longer listening. He didn't want to go to

Nombre de Dios; he wanted to go to Durango. He had to get away from this bunch, this renegade jackass with the sainted mother.

A cold thought passed through his mind: Howland had taken his money when he took his ID card, even though he'd later returned his card. Where could he get some money? he wondered. Durango, where else? Maybe he could claim the ransom money, if San Francisco sent any. If it had arrived and he could work it out, that would be some good trick.

Collect his own ransom!

Nine

The two hundred sixty-three miles from Hermosillo to Guaymas with stops at Pocitas and Cieneguita was about a seven-hour-and-forty-minute run. The day was blistering hot, the car crowded and reeking of body odor. Passengers carried live chickens in crates on their laps, men smoked rotten rope that masqueraded as cigars, an old man played a guitar badly off-key, small children bawled and shrilled, a pig got loose in the aisle, a hulking peon accidentally shattered a window with his head, and between Pocitas and Cieneguita a woman gave birth to a baby girl. Through it all Bridget O'Rourke managed to remain unperspiring, calm, every inch a lady. Ben got the impression that they were the only two people in the entire car, despite the interminable racket, the mingling of disagreeable odors, turmoil, and tightly packed passengers.

The scenery was not nearly as pleasant as she had touted it coming down through the Sonoran desert, apart from occasional picturesque villages and hamlets. The closer they drew to Guaymas, the closer they came to the sea; the land grew more fertile and as a result pleasing to view.

Bridget was a superb conversationalist; Bert would have described her as not having a giddy bone in her body. Ben guessed she was around twenty-seven but it could have been three or four years either way. She was fond of jasmine. He was most appreciative; it served admirably to ward off the more obnoxious odors that lingered in the car despite the open windows encouraging them to escape. She talked at length about her husband. Had he not been an educator, Ben would have taken him for a revolutionary—in theory, at any rate. Not the sort who secretly plots to overthrow the government with guns and bombs but an ardent advocate of change, willing to drag his soapbox anywhere at any time to preach the virtues of that change.

"A true champion of the underdog. He despised Maximillian and idolized Juarez," she said, laughing lightly. And a little sadly, thought Ben.

"Sean fought his revolution over the dinner table, his weapons his ideas, his loyal followers his students," Bridget said. "Of course, that was back when he taught history, before he became regent. When he was appointed regent, he found he had to bridle his fervor. That was after Juarez died. He died of apoplexy, you know, but Sean always said it was a broken heart. But listen to me, why must you be bored all the way to Durango with Mexican politics?"

"I'm not in the least bored. Whatever you want to talk about, I'll listen."

"Spoken like a true gentleman."

She was staring at him. She was very beautiful, he thought, and desirable. And here he was, far from anywhere familiar, separated from Bert, worried sick about his father. That is, he would have been, had it not been for her, her smile, and the jasmine.

"I notice you never talk about yourself," she said. "Do you have a murky, mysterious past?"

"Just dull. Banking is, by and large, acutely boring."

"You'd rather not talk about your—what shall I call it—mission?"

"There's nothing very secret about it. My bank is backing a new shipping venture, West coast ports in the States and in Mexico, connecting with Japan. I'm looking for financing. We have some connections in Durango, Mexico City, Vera Cruz."

"Then you won't be in Durango long."

"A week or so."

She seemed disappointed, then she brightened. "You must steal at least one day and let me show you around. It's really a fascinating place. It's the seat of a bishop, you know, and there's a bullring. We shall go to the fights together."

"That would be nice, I've never seen a bullfight."

A chicken squawked loudly in its crate across the aisle, drawing the attention of both of them. A man about Bert's age, wearing his unkempt mustache, sat holding it in his lap. *Hang on to life, Bert*, he thought. *I'm coming. It won't be long now.* . . .

Ten

Suarez's captain's uniform was practically new, although badly wrinkled. Bert had no need to ask how he'd come by it. The two bullet holes in the back were both edged with dried blood. Bert's own uniform was suitably nondescript in comparison: no epaulets, no rank stripes, plain olive drab, the button missing from one breast pocket. Suarez even added a sword to complement his two pistols.

He advised Bert that the two of them would stroll boldly into town.

"Officers always walk about like they own the place. The higher the rank, the more exaggerated the strut."

"This is crazy," complained Bert. "With this face, this skin, who's gonna take me for a Mex soldier?"

"For a *gringo* Mex soldier. Lots of *gringos* come down here and join the army. The food is poor and the pay is low, but they get to keep some of what they loot." He waggled a finger under his nose. "Just act like a soldier: Don't try anyteeng soldiers don't do to draw attention to yourself."

"I should have a gun."

"*Ayudantes de campo* don't carry arms. Hey, I tell you what I do for you. We get hold of Herbeert's boot, I get the map, I let you walk away a free man, eh? You like that? I could shoot you and leave you in a *callejuela*, but that wouldn't be fair. After all, you're doing me a favor. I return the favor. My sainted mother taught me always to be fair to my fellow man, even if he's a Yanqui. What's the matter? Walking away does not appeal to you? You rather stay weeth us? You can, just say the word."

Bert wasn't even listening. They had left the others in a grove of trees about two hundred yards from the edge of town. They had entered Nombre de Dios and were walking down the main street. Uppermost in Bert's mind at the moment was neither Howland's fictional heel and map nor Suarez's offer to join his gang, but escape. They passed an alley. The far end was in shadow, so he could not tell whether or not it was a through way to the backyards. If he made a dash in any direction, Suarez wouldn't shoot him, not in front of all these witnesses.

Wouldn't he? He might drop him in his tracks, calmly blow the smoke from his muzzle, and inform anyone interested in listening that the dead man was an escaped prisoner who had disguised himself as a soldier. His men had captured him, and he was bringing him in to be locked up. Bert could hardly argue it.

Suarez stopped them in front of a large, gloomy-looking building with a small brass sign to the right of the narrow front door: DESPITO DE CADAVARES. He walked in boldly, his sword bouncing lightly by his side. To his credit he looked every inch a military man; his posture was superb. He had lit up a crooked little cigar. He stopped in front of the reception table and blew smoke over the head of the little, harassed-looking man seated there.

"Can I help you?"

"Captain Miguel Unamano of the fourth," Suarez said. "My men brought in four corpses early thees afternoon. The *bandidos* who robbed the bank. I need to examine them so I can complete my report."

"You're out of luck."

"Eef you need a written authorization, eet is coming from Durango but won't be here until tomorrow morning. I have to leave for Villa Union tonight, colonel's orders. I will be gone for the next seex days. Now is the only time I have. First I would like to see the body of the reengleader, the *norteamericano*. On your feet, fellow, time is pressing."

"Time is always pressing for somebody or something. But you are wasting your time."

"Didn't I just explain?" rasped Suarez. "What is your name?"

"Leopoldo Maria de Ayala."

"Write that down," snapped Suarez to Bert.

Bert instinctively began fumbling in his pockets for pencil and paper. Suarez snatched both from the table, shoving them against his chest.

"Write also that we have been blocked from carrying out our offeecial duties by this fellow. Note the time of day; all offeecial complaints must carry the time of day."

If his words upset the man, he failed to show it. He calmly fished a cigarette from his pocket and lit it with a kitchen match.

"It's four o'clock," he said. "You're wasting your time because they took those stiffs away an hour ago."

"What? Why didn't you say so in the first place, you netweet!"

"You didn't give me a chance, you nitwit!"

The clerk waved them from him and resumed reading his newspaper. Suarez started to say something but changed his mind and stomped out. Bert followed. They stood outside. Suarez threw away his cigar angrily.

"Ya blew it," said Bert. "By this time they gotta have got his clothes off and his boots. They got the map."

"They got notheeng! You don't know what you're talking about. These people all move like slugs. They delivered the stiffs to Durango, *si*, and there they lay untouched. Knowing how they operate, they won't get around to tending to them for another two days, unteel they start to steenk."

Death In Durango

"They searched them two minutes after they were brought in, you betcha."

"Of course. You take me for a fool? You think I don't know that? Searched them, *si*, took their money, their valuables, but overlooked the hollow boot heel, you betcha. Who hides things in *compartimaientos* in heels, eh? Who would ever suspect?"

"All right, so we go to Durango, we check it out. We find their corpses there, but naked as jaybirds, with their clothes and his boots still here, you betcha."

"Back inside."

"You again?" exclaimed Leopoldo Maria de Ayala. "What now?"

"I weesh to examine the clothing removed from the *bandidos* before the bodies were taken to Durango. Their clothes were taken off, and they were wrapped in winding sheets, no? That's the procedure, isn't eet?"

"Please wait here."

He walked down the narrow corridor painted bile-green and vanished through the end door. Suarez fidgeted impatiently, shifting his weight from one foot to the other and back; he tried to light a fresh cigar, but the match went out before it caught. It was his last match.

"Give me a light."

"I don't smoke, I chew."

Suarez muttered under his breath and flung the cigar to the floor. "Where the devil is he? What the hell's going on? I don't like this. . . ."

"So let's get outta here."

"I want that boot!"

"You're right, somethin' is wrong. I smell trouble. Big."

Suarez growled and started toward the door at the end. When he got to it, he paused a moment, looked back, then wrenched it open.

"Hey!" he called. "Hey!"

Two policemen came in the front door, one so portly that he had to turn sideways and squeeze his way in after his partner. Both had their guns drawn. They took one look at Suarez at the far end and started shooting. Bert dropped to the floor. Instead of running inside, Suarez got out both his guns and returned fire. The blasting was so loud in the narrow room that Bert feared for his eardrums. It kept up until Suarez emptied one of his guns and threw it away. He had shot the fat policeman through the heart, killing him instantly. His partner fought on, but Suarez shot him in the hip. He dropped his gun, covering his wound with both hands and bellowing in pain.

"Come down here!" roared Suarez to Bert.

"You go ahead, I'll catch up—" he started to say, but Suarez fired one singing past his ear. "Okay, okay! You are the touchiest—"

Bert ran up to him. Suarez grabbed his shoulder and pushed him through the door. Two more policemen, followed by four others, came boiling in the front way, firing as they came. Inside the end door, Suarez pulled Bert down as he dropped, himself. A dozen slugs slammed chest-high through the closed door.

The room smelled strongly of ammonia, combined with the sickly sweet odor of formaldehyde. Bert's stomach, still empty, turned. Suarez had risen to his knees at the side of the door to lock it.

"Let's go."

Partially and completely exposed corpses lay about on tables. The impression was that morticians had been at work when the shooting started and fled. His gun still in hand, Suarez poked about.

"Maybe his boots did go with him to Durango," suggested Bert. "This is crazy. We should get gettin' outta here before they cover the back if they haven't already."

"Shut up and help look."

"You're crazy, he recognized ya, called the cops. In thirty seconds every one in town'll be surroundin' this place. You're dead, *Jefe*!"

"And you weeth me."

"They don't want me, they don't even know me."

Suarez had come up close to him. He was afraid; Bert could see it in his eyes. He suddenly seemed torn between staying and searching and getting out. Now or never, Bert thought, as he ducked and swung his right hand, catching the gun with his wrist, knocking it from Suarez's grasp. Suarez cursed him and went down after it. Bert kicked it well out of reach and ran for the back door. Outside in the yard, he paused to get his bearings. A voice growled in his left ear.

"Alzar su manos!"

"Aw, for cripes..."

He raised his hands. Two policemen came up, handcuffed him, and marched him off.

"I'm not the one! Ya want him—Suarez! He's still in here, ya dummies! I haven't done anythin'! Whatta ya doin', what's the charge?"

Neither understood a word he said. He glanced back at the half-opened rear door. Two more policemen were starting inside, moving cautiously, guns ready. Suarez would continue shooting it out, he was sure. He was that hotheaded.

"That pigheaded..."

He was a dead man, and in dying, he took Bert's alibi with him. They were heading up the alley now toward the street. He recalled that unlike American justice, wherein the burden of proof was on the accuser, in Mexico it worked the opposite way.

Eleven

Ben said his temporary farewells to Bridget O'Rourke upon arriving in Durango. He resolved to move about cautiously in light of the presumed presence of his would-be assassin. He even considered donning a disguise but dismissed the idea. Examining the situation identified three possibilities: one, Cutler had never arrived there; two, he had and Bert had already disposed of him; and three, he had arrived and disposed of Bert.

"Oh, Lord."

There was a fourth possibility. Cutler was in town, as was Bert, and the two had yet to run into each other.

The first order of business was to find Bert. Durango surprised Ben. Bridget had told him it was the largest city in the state, but he had no idea it was half the size of San Francisco. It was also called Ciudad de Victoria. It had been built in the beautiful Guidana valley formed by easterly spurs of the Sierra Madre and was nearly seven thousand feet above sea level. It had earned its rank among Mexico's more successful centers of population by virtue of the silver and iron mines in the vicinity. It boasted a handsome cathedral and no fewer than eight parish churches, a national institute where Sean O'Rourke had been regent before his death, an episcopal seminary, government buildings, a public library, a modern hospital, the state penitentiary, and the bullring Bridget had mentioned.

There were ore-reduction facilities, iron foundries, a glass works, tanneries, flour mills, sugar refineries, and two tobacco factories. The population exceeded twenty-two thousand.

Ben took a room at the Victoria Hotel. It was on the fourth floor overlooking the central plaza where pigeons and people flocked around the fountain. Curiously, the room smelled faintly of jasmine. He imagined Bridget had glided through it, trailing her favorite perfume. He wanted very much to see her again, but he must keep his priorities straight. First on the list was to find Bert.

Surprised by the size of the city, Ben had no idea where to start looking. He decided to stop by the bank to check on the ransom money. The last thing James Hume had told him about it before he boarded the *Pacific Queen* was to mention that a letter of credit had been sent from the Crocker Bank to the Banco de Mexico. The letter would have to be signed for by Bert before the ten thousand dollars could be paid. His captors would have to keep him alive at least until they collected. Then let him go? Ben didn't want to speculate on that.

A tall, urbane-looking, white-haired gentleman, who in another time and another Spanish-speaking place might have been a don, greeted him. Yes, he knew about the letter of credit; yes, it had arrived and was in the vault.

"Still? You mean no one came to collect on it?"

"Not yet."

"It's been over a week."

"Not a soul. Perhaps today, tomorrow morning. Something may have happened."

"The man who was kidnapped is my father."

"Oh, dear, I am sorry to hear it, but I did not mean that

something has happened to him. Not necessarily. It is only that the mountains are infested with outlaws. The police have their hands so full that the army has had to assist them. There are perhaps two hundred, maybe even three hundred, separate bands. What do you call them?"

"Gangs."

"They fight among themselves. Did they contact you by telegraph?" Ben nodded. "Did the sender identify himself?"

"No, but neither would I. Would you?"

The man was trying to be helpful, but nothing helpful seemed to be coming out of the conversation.

"I did a lot of thinking about it on the way down," continued Ben, "and one thing strikes me. Whoever kidnapped him knew him, at least knew he worked for Wells Fargo. And there's more. We've run up against hundreds of outlaws over the years. He's in his forties and started as a shotgun rider at sixteen before the war, so he's probably run into half the criminal population of the West. Many of them flee over the border when things get too hot.

"I think whoever kidnapped him knew him from some previous run-in, knows how good a detective he is, and that it's worth that kind of money to Wells Fargo to get him back alive. Going through his wallet and just reading his ID card wouldn't tell them that."

"So they already knew him. It sounds reasonable. You should talk to the police. They must have a list of North Americans or know people who know who they are."

Ben smiled. "Stool pigeons."

"Yes, *soplar*."

• • • •

The police sergeant introduced him to the precinct captain. He was roly-poly with a smile that stretched from one oversize ear to the other. He looked more like a pig farmer than the law. He looked like he'd slept in his uniform, but appearances proved to be deceiving. Apart from being a first-rate professional, he spoke perfect English.

"Name?"

"Bert, Egbert Slaughter. He's a detective with the Wells Fargo Express Company."

"Never heard of him."

Ben explained about the kidnapping and his feeling that an old "friend" was responsible. Even before he could finish, Captain Sidonia began to rattle off American names. "Herbert Howland, Joseph McGraw, Charlie Frydenborg, George—"

"Wait, wait, did you say Howland?"

"Herbert Howland. English, talks very strangely, wears a derby, lots of rings. We've been after him six or seven months."

"I know him. My father told me all about him. He put him behind bars for four years for robbing the Boulder, Colorado, depot. Herbert Howland."

"There are others. He may not be the only one he knew."

A policeman came in with a drunk, bringing the stink of bad whiskey with them. The man was singing incoherently. He was half dragged down the hall. The captain added six or seven more names to the list. None stirred any memories. Only Howland.

"It makes sense," Ben said. "Bert helped put him away; he'd know how good he was at his job, how valuable to the company. And given the chance to get even—"

"He's dead," said Sidonia bluntly.

"What!"

"Howland and his men were wiped out by another gang." He told Ben about the Nombre de Dios bank robbery, the outlaws' flight, and the police and the army finally catching up with them, only to find that other outlaws had gotten there first.

"Whoever it was massacred them and took the silver they had stolen."

"Bert was killed!"

"I don't think he was one of them. There were only four, Howland and his three regulars."

Two policemen walked by the open door of the little office. He jumped up and called to them. They stuck their heads in. There was a rapid exchange in Spanish. The only words Ben could understand were *pit* and *man*.

"Pit?" he asked when the others walked away.

"The three Pittman brothers from Texas. Howland and the three of them were killed. No, I really don't think your father was with them. If he was, I suppose he could have gotten away during the fighting, but from what I heard it was a bloodbath. A squirrel couldn't have gotten out alive. Perhaps he was a prisoner somewhere at the time, or back at Howland's hideout. Perhaps Howland was giving Wells Fargo time to respond to his ransom demands. Who can say what went on in the mind of a man now dead, right? But it does seem safe to say that your father wasn't with them."

"I just hope and pray he's still alive. Where's Howland's hideout?"

"Ha, if we knew that, we would have caught him ages ago. Pick any place within a radius of twenty or thirty miles, and if you find it, it'll be empty. They always are. They always seem to smell us coming. And, of course, they do move around a lot. They hit, they run. It appears that you have a high mountain to climb. I hope you find him. What is your father doing down here, looking for somebody?"

Ben nodded.

"Not Howland. Another outlaw?"

Again he nodded.

"Have you lost your tongue? I mean, I answer your questions. Can't you reciprocate?"

"Rance Cutler."

"I don't know the name. I hope they don't find each other in this district, in town, and turn the central plaza into a shooting gallery."

"Bert wouldn't do that."

"Well, if you do find him, do me a favor: Tell him to take it back up north to settle it. We've got enough homegrown trouble without having to import it."

His expression suddenly reminded Ben of James Hume's, the same sympathetic, caring, good-natured smile. Ben rose from his chair.

"I appreciate your help, Captain Sidonia."

"Now you're going out to look for your father? Not in those clothes, I hope. Get something shabby—old boots, an old hat—and leave the bulk of your money in your hotel room. You go out wandering around these mountains alone, you're sure to bump into one or another welcoming committee. The less you have on you, the less they'll take. If you look really down on your luck, they'll probably leave you alone."

"Thanks for the tip."

"One more thing. If you intend to carry a gun, keep it out of sight. Good day, Mr. Slaughter, good hunting. If I hear anything that can help you, I'll leave word at the front desk of the Victoria."

"Thanks."

● ● ● ●

Outside the police station, Ben paused to light a Jersey cheroot. It occurred to him that he should have brought along a couple plugs of Battle Ax for Bert; when he caught up with him, a peace offering would be in order. Bert had to assume he was following him down, but that didn't make him any more welcome. He checked his watch against the clock in the window of the jewelry store across the street. Twenty-eight past six. The sun was lowering, spreading a brilliant orange glow across the horizon, burnishing the bellies of the clouds hanging motionless above it. It was as if they had stopped by to warm themselves, he mused. It was too late to start searching. Better he go to bed early, get up early, and spend all day tomorrow. In line with Sidonia's suggestion he would get hold of some old clothes and a horse that looked as if it wasn't worth stealing. He would also get a map of the area, divide it into blocks, and cover each one thoroughly before moving on to the next.

With Howland and his henchmen dead no one would be claiming the ransom money now. Though Bert might—such a move on his part bordered on the outrageous, but if he was free and found himself short of cash... Ben had long ago learned never to put anything past his father.

He bought his clothes and the map on the way back to the hotel. In his room he freshened up, then kicked off his boots and sat on the bed. The faint scent of jasmine had vanished. Had Bridget O'Rourke? Time was too precious to spend even ten minutes of it dallying with her. He must find Bert before he found Cutler. He sighed. How many times had this scenario been played before? How many more to come before the issue was settled?

He lit another cheroot and went out onto his little balcony to relax and watch the activity around the fountain below. Old couples occupied the stone benches, young lovers strolled arm in arm, small children played and waded in the fountain, and the pigeons seemed to come from all over the city to clutter the area. Beyond the plaza restaurants, shops, and stalls were wedged together as far as he could see up and down the street. Every table of one sidewalk café was occupied. His eyes moved from one to the next and stopped.

A man in a black suit was sitting with his back to him. As Ben spotted him he turned to his right—he was wearing an eye patch. Ben recognized him even as he turned back, his profile vanishing. Recognized the set of his shoulders; his broad back; his dark hair, usually worn shoulder length, now cut short.

Cutler!

He was wearing, of all things, a clerical collar. Also a full beard. But it was Cutler—no mistake. Opposite him, her slender hand wrapped around a glass, sat Bridget O'Rourke.

Twelve

The cell was a pesthole. Two dead rats hosting legions of fleas lay on the floor when the guard unlocked the door to admit Bert. The guard obligingly removed the two corpses; Bert squashed all the fleas he could see under his heel. The paper-thin blanket on the narrow cot smelled of mildew. The walls were wet to the touch; a candle, his only source of light since there was no window, had been reduced to a stump less than an inch high; and a half bucket of dirty water looked to be all he would have to wash with. He complained bitterly, and to save his eardrums from undue punishment the guard disposed of the water and brought him fresh.

He still had not eaten. Supper was not for two more hours, but the guard gave him the half of taco left from his own noon meal. It was cold and stale, but Bert downed every morsel. There was nothing to drink but the wash water.

He demanded to see the head jailer. He put up such a

fuss, the guard finally relented and went to fetch him. When he appeared, to Bert's surprise and chagrin he looked enough like Suarez to be his brother, or at least a cousin.

"What's all the foos?" he asked in badly broken English.

"The 'foos' is ya got the wrong man! I'm innocent! He forced me at gunpoint to dress up like this and go with him to check the stiffs. I didn't have any gun! That slimy snake, Howland, left me tied up in his cabin, Suarez and his bunch found me, woulda killed me on the spot if I hadn't'a talked 'em out of it with a cock-and-bull story. Which is why he went there, to find Howland's corpse and his boots. I told him Howland kept a map to where he hid all the silver he stole in the heel o' his boot. It's baloney, but he b'lieved it and took me along when he went lookin' for the map. So ya can plainly see I'm a pure victim o' circumstances. He as good as held a rope 'round my neck—had a gun at my back, that's for sure."

"What is your name?"

"Bert Wallace Arlo Slaughter. I'm a detective with Wells Fargo; you savvy Wells Fargo? Biggest express comp'ny in the world. I'm down here after a bad actor by the name o' Rance Cutler. He's hangin' 'round Durango, least that's what my information is."

"You are a detective?"

"In the flesh. Sixteen years."

"You have identification?"

"You betcha!" Bert brightened. He reached for his wallet; the grin slid from his face. "In my other drawers, back at Suarez's hideout. Howland took my wallet, took my money, but I walked him into givin' me back my wallet with my ID. I had to have it to identify myself when I went with him to collect my ransom."

"What are you talking about?"

"Nothin', nothin', that's a whole other story. Only I haven't got my wallet on me, it's in my other pants back at Suarez's. Cross my heart hope to die, I am what I say I am."

"You are an army deserter who linked up with him."

"Like hell! That's crazy! He forced me to put this on. I

keep tellin' ya, I was his pris'ner. Your boys caught him, they musta, they had that place surrounded. He was runnin' outta ammunition—"

"He got away."

"He what! That's impossible! He couldn' have! He musta bribed some o' the cops. What kinda police force ya got 'round here, anyhow?"

"He bribed nobody. When the shooting started, the morticians working in the back room ran upstairs to hide. When the shooting stopped, one of them foolishly came back down. His curiosity very nearly cost him his life. It well may have by now. Suarez took him hostage. He was an old man; the police were helpless. Suarez demanded a horse be brought for him. They stood by, powerless, and watched him ride off with his hostage."

"Great! Wonderful! Some fine kettle o' fish! He's free, and here I am holdin' the damn sack! Ya gotta let me outta here, I mean now!"

"I'm afraid that's impossible. You claim you're innocent. In light of what happened, your association with a known criminal, you appear to be guilty. Another army deserter gone wrong. It is for the courts to decide. All we can do is hold you."

"All right, all right. Look, do this much. Send a telegram for me to the Wells Fargo Express Company, San Francisco, California. To Mr. James B. Hume. Tell him what's happened. Tell him I said to get in touch with the American ambass'dor in Mexico City, okay?"

The jailer's face fell. "The American ambassador?"

Mention of the title seemed to make him nervous. From his point of view the situation rapidly was getting out of hand. Bert took note of his reaction. He was overloading the man. What was he, after all, but a provincial jailer, a low-paid public servant with limited authority and limited intelligence and imagination to complement it.

"Just do one thing. Give me pencil and paper and let me write down 'zackly what to put into the wire."

The jailed hesitated, licking his lips, furrowing his brow. He then nodded to the guard. Pencil and paper were brought.

Bert sat mulling over precisely what he wanted to say while both men stood outside staring at him. Their attitudes had changed drastically since he'd mentioned the ambassador. Both seemed afraid of him. He finally got his thoughts down clearly and in proper sequence:

> JAMES STOP SOS STOP HELD PRISONER NOMBRE DE DIOS JAIL STOP CASE OF MISTAKEN IDENTITY OR SOMETHING STOP HAVE BEEN CAPTIVE BY SOMEBODY OR OTHER EVER SINCE I GOT HERE STOP ALERT AMERICAN AMBASSADOR IN MEXICO CITY TO GET ME OUT OF HERE STOP DESPERATE STOP DONT TELL BEN WHERE I AM BS STOP

He handed the message to the jailer. "Get it off quick as you can, okay?"

"Who will pay?"

"Send it collect. There's no time to lose. And get me some hot food, can'tcha? And coffee. And make it hot. And some flea powder for the floor. And get me a decent blanket. And a pillow. Soft. And I need a new candle. Make it a couple. And send somebody back to Suarez's hideout to get my clothes. Like I said, my wallet's in the back pocket o' my drawers. Tell whoever you send to guard my ID with his life. And how 'bout a clean towel and some soap?"

Neither man responded or even looked back at him as they walked away. The jailer was muttering. He appeared to be complaining to the guard.

• • • •

The sight of Bridget O'Rourke deep in friendly conversation with none other than Rance Cutler stunned Ben. He didn't know what to make of it, apart from the obvious fact that there was a good deal more to Bridget than she had elected to show him. Seated at the table, having cocktails, they looked as if they'd known each other for years. Was that possible? She had come down from Portland where she claimed she was visiting her sister-in-law. On the train she'd talked about everything imaginable except, now that he thought about it, Portland and her visit, the reason for her trip north. Seeing her with Cutler shattered his image of her. Everything about her was suddenly open to question: her politics, her claims for her late husband, her professed friendship with the bank president.

"What is God's name is she doing with Cutler?" he asked himself out loud for the fourth time, sitting on his bed and staring at his image in the glass over the washbasin.

One thing was certain: He must do his best to avoid her. Again he went out onto his balcony. They were still sitting, chatting. The waiter brought the check. Cutler fumbled in his pocket; she reached out and stopped his hand and paid the bill herself. He watched them get up, still talking animatedly. They stood outside the café railing. Ben put his boots back on and ran three flights down to the lobby. By the time he got outside, she was nowhere to be seen. Cutler was walking briskly up the street. He'd added a cane to his disguise, which Ben hadn't noticed while he was at the table.

He ran after him. He followed for a couple of blocks, but Cutler's stride was long and he stayed well ahead. He crossed a side street, but when Ben reached the curb in pursuit, a large horse-drawn van turned into the street, blocking the way completely. He ran out into the main street to peer around the end of the van. He could see Cutler in the crowd. Ben was nearly struck by a Victoria carrying two old ladies and was shouted at by a policeman before he managed to get around the van into the next block. By the time he did, Cutler had vanished.

"Damn!"

All wasn't lost, he mused. At least he hadn't left town, and it stood to reason that if he'd already shot it out with Bert and beaten him, he'd have left. Or would he have? *He* hadn't come to Durango to confront Bert; it was the other way around. Cutler's only reason for being there was to do business with Bridget O'Rourke, so it seemed.

Should he take her up on her invitation to act as his

guide? Certainly she had no idea he'd seen her with Cutler. Strolling about town with her in friendly, meaningless conversation, he might succeed in tricking her into betraying what she and Cutler were up to. No, she was too clever for that. If she wanted him to know, she would have said something on the train. If he wanted to find out what was going on, the information would have to come from another source. As far as that went, why should he even bother? Just to appease his curiosity? He had better things to do.

Nevertheless, he couldn't help wondering. The sight of them together had astonished him. He'd yet to recover from it.

• • • •

It was past eight-thirty. Durango's lights gleamed prettily; nightlife was in full swing. Ben found a small restaurant across the street from the National Institute. He sat by himself at a corner table, sipping a local rum drink recommended by the waiter. It proved too sweet for him, but he didn't complain to the man for fear of hurting his feelings. Tourists in general were a heavy-handed and outspoken lot, and he was not about to assume the caricature of them as seen through the eyes of the locals.

A balding, middle-aged man sat alone at the next table. Every other table in view was occupied by two or more patrons. As often happens, the two solitary diners, seated less than two feet from each other, struck up a conversation. The man introduced himself as Professor Francisco Rondaliego. A nervous tic animated his left cheek just under his eye, and he breathed loudly and moistly through his generous nose. He was plain-faced, with no outstanding characteristics other than his tic and his manner of breathing, but Ben found him very friendly and his English remarkable, better than Captain Sidonia's by a wide margin. He taught economics at the National Institute. This he told Ben offhandedly, almost apologetically. It straightened Ben in his chair.

"How interesting," he said.

"Oh, not very, not after twenty-three years. Yes, it's

twenty-three years this week since I joined the faculty. I'll be retiring in two years. It's mandatory, you know."

"You don't look old enough to retire."

"You flatter me." His eyes twinkled. "How old do you think I am?"

"I can't possibly guess, fifty-five, six?"

"Sixty-three!"

"Amazing. You don't look even close to sixty."

"I take good care of myself. A couple pounds overweight, perhaps, but healthy. Hale and hearty, that's me. I must say I don't look forward to retirement. I'm a bachelor; I plan to travel extensively, but I'll miss the classroom. It's like a comfortable pair of shoes that are all worn-out but which you don't want to get rid of."

"Twenty-three years..."

"This week."

"I came down on the train with a lovely young lady, a widow. Her late husband was regent at the institute. Sean O'Rourke?"

"Sean O'—" Professor Rondaliego burst out laughing, so loudly that conversation cut off at tables all around them. Two waiters standing on the far side of the room with their trays under their arms and napkins over their arms reacted, startled. "Oh, dear me, I apologize. Such a spectacle I've made...."

"What's so funny?"

"Sean O'Rourke regent? Who on earth told you such a thing?"

"His wife."

"My dear fellow, if it's the Sean O'Rourke I know, he was no closer to regent than the janitor. He was an obscure history teacher. I say obscure, but I don't mean it derogatorily. Still, that's what he was. He only lasted seven months. Came out of nowhere and, for all I know, went back to nowhere. Yes, he did die. Sean O'Rourke—my, my, my, talk about names out of the past. The funny thing is that he was an excellent teacher."

"He was only there seven months? What happened?"

"What did he cause to happen, you mean? What didn't

he?'' Rondaliego looked both ways and lowered his voice. "The man was a revolutionary, ardent, a positive fanatic. He'd stand up in class and make interminable speeches in praise of President Juarez, and when he died and President Lerdo took his place, O'Rourke's tongue turned into a flaming sword. He lost all perspective. I mean, what history teacher doesn't go off the deep end with his political opinions once in a while? It's something of an addiction with that lot, but O'Rourke...

"Understand something, I genuinely liked him; he was extraordinarily bright, very witty—I envy a good sense of humor—and, as I said, a superb teacher. He just had no control. Like most colleges and universities, the National Institute is a breeding ground for ideas, as liberal as any place, regardless of how bizarre or anarchic or outrageous one's notions may strike others. There's always somebody who'll listen and agree, but he went much too far. The board warned him. They were very patient with him, but it only seemed to encourage him to go further. They finally had no choice but to fire him."

"After only seven months."

"Smack in the middle of the second term. Personally I always thought"—Rondaliego lowered his voice even further—"he was a little crazy, perhaps more than a little. I've never seen such deliberate self-destruction. He was no stripling, you know; he was almost fifty when he came to work here. Strange chap, a gentleman terrorist when it came to politics, that's the only way to describe him. Politics consumed him, his special brand. Benito Juarez was his personal saint. When Juarez died, Sean fell to pieces. He railed against every other presidential candidate as unworthy—to him one and all were cretins, perverts, the dregs of the barrel." He paused to sip. "His wife actually told you he was regent? Sean O'Rourke regent? Priceless!"

"From the way she spoke, they seemed very devoted to each other."

"I'm sure they were, despite the difference in their ages. She *is* much younger, isn't she? I met her only once. She's quite an eyeful and bright, not one of those empty-headed dolls, but I remember coming away from that affair thinking there was something mystical about her.'' He nodded, agreeing with himself. ''Mystical. With what you might call overtones of fanaticism. I'm sure she shared his political views, only she was no ranter and raver.''

By now they were sharing the same table, Rondaliego helping Ben transfer his utensils, plates, and glasses, and ignoring the waiters' quizzical looks. Both finished the meal with an aperitif. Ben insisted on picking up the check. It seemed only fair; after all, Educator Francisco Rondaliego had spent nearly the past two hours educating him, and without charge. Only one small cloud hung over the enlightening evening: the fact that the professor did not know Bridget better. Still, what he knew of her husband told Ben enough about the lady to change his view of her drastically.

Bridget and Cutler, Cutler and Bridget; a strange couple. And what was he doing disguised as a cleric? He wasn't wanted in Mexico. American law couldn't lay hands on him down here, so why the disguise? For her benefit? Or at her suggestion?

What was going on?

Thirteen

Bert awoke from a troubled and fitful sleep to his fifth day behind bars. The last shred of his patience had deserted him two days before. Under the best of circumstances patience was not one of his strong suits; under these there was no place for it. He had been in jail before, more than once guilty of the charge against him and deserving of incarceration, but never before had he seen the inside of a Mexican cell, despite having visited the country no fewer than seven times previously. His cell was no dirtier than the one in Abilene or his thirteen-day residence in Butte; no smaller than the one in Sante Fe, neither darker nor danker than the ones in Silver City, Idaho, and Vicksburg, Arizona; but this was a Mexican cell, and Mexican justice had a reputation for being quick and harsh. During tumultuous times the rifle barrels of the firing squads had little time to cool; the country seemed to be overrun with *bandidos;* the mountains around Durango certainly were. Politicians were outraged, the people angry, the police frustrated. Renegades like Suarez roamed free, seemingly immune to arrest. The few who were caught were dealt with harshly, the authorities overcompensating for their ineffectualness. He had been caught. That he was a genuine victim of circumstances didn't matter to those outside the bars; the burden was on him to prove his innocence, and clearly nobody—not the guards, not the jailer, not the man on the street—preferred that he be innocent. All wanted him punished, all wanted him dead; one more step toward restoration of law and order.

They're gonna shoot ya, Slaughter. They don't wanna listen, they don't wanna know the true facts, they just want ya dead. They won't even let ya choose between the firin' squad and the noose. Ya gotta get outta here.

The early-shift guard, who went off duty at eight A.M., came in with his breakfast: cold beans, bread as hard as the pommel of a saddle, and lukewarm coffee. Breakfast never varied, apart from the number of beans he was served. There appeared to be five or six more than usual this morning. What were they doing, he wondered, fattening him up for the kill? Breakfast was also supper. Lunch was different—there was generally a thin broth or soup and a piece of fruit.

The guard looked about fifteen. His uniform was two sizes too big for him, and he bunched his shirt in the back, stuffing the excess material into his belt to better fill out the front with his scrawny chest. He wore a perpetual gloomy expression. He was, decided Bert, either unlucky in love or suffering chronic stomach distress. He couldn't tell which, and he didn't care. His only interest in him was that of the three guards he appeared most vulnerable. His eyes announced that his mind was not on his work. Time and again bringing Bert's meal in, he carelessly offered the hip his gun was holstered to. Bert had spent four days weighing the pros and cons of attempting to escape. He concluded that staying would be suicide.

But when the guard appeared, bearing his breakfast tray, Bert's face and heart fell as one. Overnight the guard had acquired a new holster for his pistol, army-issue, featuring a flap with a strap that buckled over his grip.

"Cripes' sake," muttered Bert.

The guard greeted him unsmilingly. Both hands occupied with the tray, he had elbowed open the door to the office, leaving it ajar. Bert nodded and cocked an ear toward the office. If the jailer had arrived, either he had fallen asleep at his desk or was reading; it was possible he hadn't come in to work yet, but that was a chance Bert would rather not take.

"Wouldya shut the door?" he asked the guard. The man stared, clearly not understanding him. "Ah, closo the *porto*." He gestured.

"Ah, *puerta*."

"*Si*. There's a draft. Drafto. Coldo!"

He wrapped his arms around his chest and shivered. The guard shrugged and closed the door. Two other prisoners occupied cells: a drunk who had been brought in the night before singing at the top of his lungs and promptly vomiting all over his cell; and a little man who looked like a balding ferret and had given himself up after shooting his mistress and his wife, killing one, wounding the other. Both were awake, both looked longingly at Bert's breakfast. Bert looked at it disdainfully. You're welcome to it, he thought.

Balancing the tray on one hand, the guard unlocked his door. He handed him the tray. Bert set it on the cot. He held up his left hand, palm forward.

"Hando, *mano,* sore, bustedo..."

The guard gaped stupidly. Up came Bert's right, cold-cocking him. He reacted with surprise bordering on shock, grunted, and sank slowly to the floor.

"Let me out! Let me out!" burst the cold-sober drunk.

"Shut up, ya jackass!" hissed Bert. "Keep your shirt on, lemme get organized here."

He got out the guard's pistol. It was empty. He loaded it from his belt, then went to the inner door and pressed his ear against it. He could hear what sounded like the rustling of a newspaper. Pressing his finger to his lips, the two prisoners watching his every move, he slowly opened the door a couple of inches. Then backed off.

"What kinda swill is this! What right ya got to feed a man hog sloppin's? Just 'cause I'm a pris'ner doesn't mean I got no rights!"

"Shut up your mouth, Wells Fargo, or I'll come in and stuff your rights down your miserable throat!" bawled the jailer.

"You go to hell!"

Bert hunched by the side of the door, the gun upraised, grip high. In stormed the jailer, down came the gun. He crumpled and lay still.

"Let us out!" bawled the drunk.

"Let yourselves..."

Bert snatched up the key ring and tossed it his way. It struck the bars and fell to the floor. Gun in hand, he ran out front. The man called after him.

"I can't reach 'em! Hey! Heyyyyyy!"

"Tough," muttered Bert. "Stretch farther."

He shoved the gun in his belt, dashed out the door, around the corner of the building, and down the alley. As he ran, he resolved to steal the first horse he came upon.

You're in the soup up to your neck now, friend. Whatever ya do, you can't get in any deeper....

● ● ● ●

Ben dismounted and led his horse, a flea-bitten, elderly gray mare, up to the front door of the cabin. It stood slightly ajar. He stopped, placed his hand on his gun, and listened. There was no one inside. He pushed in. The first sight to meet his eyes was the decaying remains of the deer hanging from the rafters, the source of the revolting stench now overpowering, nauseating; he pinched his nose with thumb and forefinger. The crushed remains of a scorpion lay in the middle of the floor. Nearby lay pieces of rope. A derby hung from a peg on the wall to his left. He examined it. Inside the lining he read: "Carlings for Men—Boston," and the initials H. R. H.

Herbert Howland? he wondered. Mexicans were not partial to derbies. He doubted if any outside of the larger cities ever wore one. H. R. H. Herbert R. Howland. Very possible. Probable. So this was Howland's hideout, where he'd brought Bert after he'd captured him.

Ben's glance strayed to the pieces of rope on the floor. He knelt to examine them. Howland had tied him. One of the thousand nuggets of trail smarts Bert had passed on to him over the years was that when someone tied somebody else up and later set them free, they usually didn't cut them loose. The reason for this was that they had tied them with *their* rope; *their* rope had a value to them; they were disinclined to destroy it when they could use it again. On the other hand, if a third party came along and freed Bert, they would probably cut the rope. It was faster and it wasn't their rope. Had Howland tied Bert up and left him to go bank robbing? Had whoever bushwhacked Howland and killed him come back here, found Bert, and cut him free?

It seemed likely. Only, what then? What happened from then on? Did whoever freed him kill him? Why would he? On the other hand, why let him live? Or had Bert talked him into letting him walk? Possibly; he was good at that sort of thing. Only, what had he told them to persuade them to spare him? It was all beginning to dizzy him slightly, along with the horrendous stink of the dead deer. Holding on to two pieces of the rope, he went back outside, moving out of range of the smell. He sucked his lungs full of fresh air.

He had been searching for four days. This was the first glimmer of luck but barely a glimmer. All it really told him was that Howland had held Bert prisoner here, and somebody else, most likely whoever killed Howland, had come and set him free. So up to this point he was still alive.

As was Ben himself. Captain Sidonia's warning about the perils of traipsing about the mountains alone came back to him. So far he'd been lucky—he hadn't seen a soul. Still holding the pieces of rope, he sat down on a rock to consider his next move. It didn't seem to make any sense to continue searching. For what? Unnecessary trouble was about the only thing he foresaw encountering. Was Bert back in Durango? Had he finally gotten around to tracking

Cutler? Had he, like Cutler, disguised himself? If only Durango wasn't so big, so intricate to search...

Maybe he was going about the thing all wrong; maybe he should ride back to the city and get after Cutler. Get him in his sights but not eliminate him, though how he'd love to! Instead, keep tabs on him in the hope that sooner or later he would attract Bert. Also, if he stayed in the shadows and Bert did show, he could help prevent Cutler from getting the drop on him.

Where would he find Cutler? He reached into his pocket and brought out the slip of paper on which Bridget O'Rourke had written her address. It was a house on Independence Square, number 113. He got out his map. Independence Square was seven blocks northeast of the Hotel Victoria. Maybe he could position himself out of sight across the street from the house. And wait for Cutler to come calling.

No.

Bridget would meet with him, drink with him, do business with him, but that business had to be shady. What other sort would he be involved in? So she wouldn't invite him to the house for tea, even disguised as he was. Watching her place would be a waste of time. What then?

He'd have to think about it. He tossed away the pieces of rope, mounted his horse, and headed back to the city.

● ● ● ●

There was a message for him at the front desk, a piece of notepaper folded once, no envelope. When the clerk handed it to him, he casually sniffed it for the scent of jasmine, but there was no odor. He would be slightly shocked if there had been. It was from Captain Sidonia.

"Come see me at your earliest convenience. I've heard something that may interest you."

"What?"

The desk clerk looked up from the stack of letter in his hand. His mustache was absurdly large for his slender, little face, and his pallor suggested that he never ventured out into the sun.

"Nothing," muttered Ben, "just talking to myself."

"There was another message. A boy from the Banco de Mexico stopped by this noon. He said to tell you that Mr. Pumeriega said that a man came in asking about the ransom money?" It came out as a question; the clerk looked puzzled. "He, himself, did not see him, so he doesn't know what he looked like. When he told his secretary to ask him to come in, she went back to get him and he was gone."

"Bert. He got cold feet...."

"I beg your pardon?"

"Nothing."

It had to be Bert! It couldn't be Howland. Couldn't be any of the Pittmans. Wait, it didn't have to be Bert, it could have been whoever cut him loose. He must have a word with Pumeriega's secretary. She'd be able to describe him. But first he would go and see what Sidonia had.

"Thank you very much." He waved Sidonia's note. "I have to go. I'll be back in an hour in case there are any more messages."

● ● ● ●

Captain Sidonia wasn't feeling well. He complained of having eaten a fish that didn't sit well. He tried to smile through his discomfort. He kept rubbing his stomach and grimacing.

"An interesting development, Mr. Slaughter. By the way, I take it you've been out searching for your father. In your travels did you happen to bump into an outlaw by the name of Profiro Suarez?"

"I haven't run into anybody."

"Lucky you."

The story of how Suarez and a companion had been trapped inside the mortuary in Nombre de Dios had reached Durango. Suarez had escaped the shoot-out; his companion had been captured.

"His description tallies with your description of your father," Sidonia said.

"Unbelievable!"

"That it's him or that he would be running with a bad customer like Suarez?"

"He must have untied him. Was it Suarez who ambushed Howland and his men?"

"I don't know. It's possible...."

"I've got to get over there. What a relief. At least now I know he's alive." He started up from his chair.

"Sit still. The police captured him, but this morning he broke jail. Knocked out the guard with his own pistol, knocked out the jailer, and got away."

"Oh, my God..."

"Last we heard they are out combing the area."

"It's stupid! What do they want with him? He hasn't done anything; he wouldn't, he's as straight as a die. This Suarez must have had him under his thumb. Did my father have a gun? I'll bet he didn't," Ben said.

Sidonia shrugged. "I'm sure the police over there aren't that interested in him. Suarez is the one they want. They see your father as a direct link to him. Perhaps they believe he'll rejoin him as soon as he can and lead them straight to him."

"That's idiotic. He'd no more run back to him—"

"Try to see it from their point of view," he interrupted. "He's all they have to go on. One thing: If they do catch up with him, they won't harm him. It's the big cheese they're after. Hey, don't look so discouraged; it's mixed news, not good but not all that bad. Like you say, at least he's alive."

"This is getting more and more bizarre: *bandidos*; a phony priest; a university regent that never was; his widow, shaped like a goddess, who lies like a rug; a cockney outlaw with a derby; a ten-thousand-dollar ransom lying unclaimed in the bank; a shoot-out in a mortuary..."

"Hey, welcome to Mehico!"

Fourteen

The first horse Bert came upon was a finer animal than he expected: a sorrel mare wearing an expensive saddle, ready and willing to run with anybody on her back. He promptly set forth for Suarez's hideout, dusting out of Nombre de Dios into the welcome concealment of the rugged mountaintop.

Then he changed his mind and headed instead for Durango, more than thirty miles away. Why not take a crack at the ransom money? he thought. What did he have to lose? If it had arrived, Howland wouldn't be claiming it, nor the Pittmans. Reaching the city, he got directions to the Banco de Mexico. The receptionist greeted him with a peculiar smile. Her eyes traveled down his uniform when he introduced himself. Then her peculiar smile gave way to a look of total confusion.

"My name's Slaughter. I want to talk to somebody about the ransom money from Wells Fargo, from San Francisco."

She walked away, moving behind the tellers' cages down to the corner office. He could see her in conversation with a woman seated at a small desk just outside the office door. The woman at the desk kept leaning over, looking past the receptionist at him.

He sighed. "What the devil? What are ya tryin' to pull?"

In his haste to get to the bank it hadn't occurred to him that he didn't have his ID on him; he couldn't begin to prove who he was, and the uniform had to make anyone he talked to suspicious. He had already confused the receptionist; the secretary wore a similar expression.

Better he get out of there, ride to the hideout, recover his clothes and wallet, and come back here, able to prove he was who he claimed to be. He left.

He gave Nombre de Dios a wide berth on the way back. He began looking for landmarks he'd filed in his memory en route to town from the hideout. The trails twisted so, meeting and crossing and petering out, that it was difficult to find the way. Suarez's best reason for selecting the place originally, he decided. He had to find it, had to get back there, had to get out of his uniform, back into his own clothes with his wallet in his pocket. His ID was his proof of innocence: Caught a second time without it, he'd be back in jail again before he could clear his throat.

After a series of wrong turns and changes in direction he finally, luckily, found the right trail and came to within about a mile of the hideout. Hopefully Suarez and his men would be out working. He could be in and out in sixty seconds if need be. He would change his clothes in the woods.

Would his wallet still be in his back pocket where he'd left it? Or had one of the men remembered it and come back to steal it? Thieving pigs, he wouldn't put it past any one of them. Had Suarez stashed any cash around the place? Maybe he should give it a quick once-over. He might get lucky; a little luck was overdue him. His latest blast of bad luck was Hume's failure to act on his telegram. Had it even been sent? He wouldn't bet on it.

A wave of relief coursed through his heart as he came within sight of the place and saw nobody about. It was about twice the size of Howland's shack and in better condition, tidier, with no deer carcass hanging from the rafters.

"Fillin' it with stink. Disgustin'...."

He dismounted about thirty yards from the front, hitching the horse to a pine tree and moving stealthily forward. He could see no sign of life, and there were no horses. Nevertheless, there was no point in taking unnecessary chances. He bypassed the front door and, walking around the side, peered through the window. The place was empty. His hat and pants and shirt still lay on the chair where he'd left them. He ran inside, picked them up, put them down, and turned to searching for money. He banged his way through the kitchen cabinets, examining pots and pails and other containers, checked behind the framed painting of a buffalo on the wall, and checked all the beds.

He failed to turn up a dime. He began checking the floor for loose boards, and those that appeared to have been tampered with. He started to sweat. He reckoned he'd been there close to half an hour, and the longer he stayed, the bigger the risk he was taking. If, God forbid, Suarez suddenly showed up, there'd be hell to pay!

Prodded by his growing anxiety and an ingrained reluctance to take foolish chances whatever the circumstances, he finally gave it up. He changed his clothes, threw the uniform into the bushes, and mounted up. He started back the way he'd come, resolving to bypass Nombre de Dios by an even wider margin than before. He could be in Durango in an hour.

Word of his escape had to have spread far and wide by now, and the police in Durango would have their eyes peeled. But hopefully for the "army deserter," not an American tourist, although he looked about as much like the latter as he did an *ayundante de campo* in the uniform.

So involved was he in pushing these thoughts around in his mind, he failed to hear the horses approaching until they were almost upon him. He snapped to attention, lifting his head.

"Wells Fargo!" rasped Suarez.

Bert swallowed so hard, he nearly cracked his throat. He

felt as if a pile driver had come plummeting down upon him. He sank in the saddle.

"'Lo..."

Suarez seemed to have every man with him. They were evidently on the way to the hideout. There was no sign of the hostage Suarez had reportedly taken. Bert fleetingly wondered if the poor man survived his ordeal, or was he presently being returned to the mortuary to be worked on by one of his associates? Would he, himself, soon be? It was seriously beginning to look like it.

Suarez leered. "You got your fancy clothes back, I see."

"You don't 'spect me to spend the rest o' my life runnin' 'round lookin' like a army deserter, do you?"

"The rest of your life may not be that long." Up came his right hand, holding a pair of boots. Again Bert swallowed too hard. "Guess who?"

"Not Howland's..."

"Howland's."

"Not his reg'lar ones, his fav'rites, not by a long shot. He musta changed."

"Shut your mouth, you liar! You have been deceiving me all along." He tapped one heel, then the other. "Solid, no *compartimiento*, no map, notheeng!"

"On account of you got the wrong boots, I tell ya! Would I lie to ya?"

"*Silencio!*" He jerked out his left gun and leveled it at Bert's face. He stiffened expectantly. "I'll blow your lying tongue through the back of your head, liar! Liar!"

"Go 'head, you'd shoot a unarmed man, me who's been through thick and thin with ya, and just spent a week in the foulest, stinkin'est, most disgustin' jail in this God-forsook country. Bein' beat and tortured to make me tell where you're at and never spillin' one bean, so help me. Protectin' ya! Helpin' ya, layin' my life on the line for ya like the good-hearted s'maritan I am. Tryin' to help you find his map to his silver, which I hope with all my heart and all my prayers you'll find, on account I hated that cockney rat so much, so fierce, any man who punches his ticket deserves all the help I can give him, which is you—"

"Stop blabbering!" the outlaw said with a sneer.

His expression of hatred seemed very intense, but he slowly lowered his gun, then jammed it back into its holster.

"I weesh they did torture you, hang you! All liars should be hung by their tongues, *gringo* peeg! *Broza!* Steenking liar! Ride ahead..."

"Where we goin'?"

"*You* are riding to your death, but before I kill you, I want to see you sweat. I never shoot a man like you dry. He must be sweating like a peeg panting in the heat, sweating buckets, drenched and dying by inches." He dropped the boots, whipped out both guns, and fired, the slugs bracketing Bert's head just below the earlobes. Suarez scowled.

"Sweat, peeg!"

Fifteen

Captain Sidonia was proving to be a reliable magnet for information. Everything that happened in the area seemed to find its way to his hearing. Ben was preparing to leave his office to go to the bank to confirm his assumption that it was Bert who had shown up earlier, when another piece of news arrived. At the behest of Governor Concepción the Mexican army had assigned a troop of cavalry, a hundred and twenty strong under a Captain Frasquita, to capture Profiro Suarez and his gang. What the area police, short of manpower and overburdened with work, appeared incapable of doing, the military would attend to. Two things the cavalry brought to the manhunt: superior horsemanship and superior weapons, principally the Winchester .44-.40 lever-action rifle, recently imported from the U.S.

"Where do I find this Frasquita?" asked Ben.

"At army headquarters on the outskirts of the city. On the Conatlán road. Why? If you're thinking about riding with them..."

"Exactly. Bert is either with Suarez, or Suarez knows where I can find him."

"My friend, I happen to know Captain Frasquita; we had a run-in about a year ago. He is one of a kind, the most obstinate man in Christendom. He goes by the book, I mean to the letter, the dot over the *i*. You ask if you can ride with them and out will come the book, open to the page, and he'll read you the rule forbidding civilians accompanying troops on assignment. Mind you, I'm not saying he's not a good soldier. He's *estaño soldado;* know what that is? Tin soldier. Wind him up, assign him, and he performs. Perfectly. Don't waste your time...."

"It's my time."

"Buena suerte."

• • • •

Captain Frasquita and his men were already mounted and preparing to ride out when Ben came barreling up. The post looked like a fastidiously wrought painting: freshly painted barracks buildings standing in a row, windows polished and shining, stoops tidily swept, flowers flanking the front doors, not a weed in sight, not a pebble. The red, green, and white Mexican flag hung limply from its pole, its base encircled with whitewashed stones encompassing a flower bed. Brass and leather, on man and horse alike, gleamed in the sunlight. Captain Frasquita's uniform looked brand-new; his brass buttons resembled gold; every strand of his epaulets hung poker-straight, in perfect alignment, suggesting that they were starched; the visor of his cap glistened like glass; the grip, haft, and trimmings of his saber in its scabbard blazed in the sunlight; his stagskin gloves displayed Mexican eagles stitched with gold thread on the backs. His mustache was freshly waxed, the ends rising to needle-sharp points; he was otherwise clean-shaven, his cheeks and chin powdered and his head and shoulders thrust into a cloud of eau de cologne. His shoulders were widened with padding, his chest barrel-full and doubtless also padded. His waist as slender as a woman's. His boots looked to be sculptured of onyx.

His men were as gleaming and perfect in appearance as he. His handsome boyish face expressed disapproval at Ben's abrupt arrival. Ben introduced himself and promised to delay their departure.

"Only a moment. Suarez is holding my father prisoner. He's in grave danger. Please let me ride with you."

"Impossible. Move clear. B troooooooop—"

"Wait, wait, please! I won't get in the way. I'll obey your every command. I just want to be there. I have to—"

"You will not. For a civilian to ride with us would be in direct contravention of general order number thirty-four, paragraph three. 'Civilian scouts only are permitted to accompany troops on patrol; no other civilians. There can be no exception to this rule.' The rule is for your protection. Now, please move your animal clear, you are delaying us. And do not attempt to follow; outriders will be posted at the rear of the column. If you are seen anywhere in the vicinity, you will be apprehended and turned over to the nearest civilian authorities. Appropriate charges will be lodged against you. Good day, sir. B troooooooop..."

● ● ● ●

"One thing: You're all mixed up, which is the whole snag here between you and me. Those boots. Howland's best boots, his fav'rites, which happen to be high tops with long mule-ear and with low heels, got to be back at his place. I 'member now they got copper-top caps, too, like the kids wear. You know how for'ners are, they never can take good, genuine, 'merican 'quipment and use it like everybody else, they got to finagle with it, rerig it."

"Sweat."

"This is *loco*, I'm your ticket to that stash, and here you want to tear me up and throw me away. For the last time, we should be ridin' for his place. The boots you're lookin' for are there, they got to be!"

"Even if we found another pair, how would we know they were hees?"

"By the compartment, for cripe's sakes, and the map inside. Man, you're not thinkin' straight!"

"I'm theenking you are lying like you've never lied before, hoping to save your worthless hide. We get to Howland's, we find no boots, nothing, and by that time, you weel have another lie. Doesn't your mouth ever get tired of talking, talking? You are wearing out all our ears!"

"What it comes down to is either ya want the silver or ya don't. If ya don't, kill me; but if ya do, ya better hadn't, you'll be sorry. You'll kick yourself the rest o' your days."

"Sweat."

They were heading north toward Conatlán and beyond it the Santiaguillo Lake country. The sky was magnificent, robin's-egg blue with not so much as a wisp of cloud. The sun off to their left burned fiercely, pouring its heat down upon Bert's shoulders and back. He was wringing with sweat; how much more did he have? he wondered. Why was Suarez keeping him alive? Had he succeeding in planting a seed of doubt in his mind? He wasn't any more sadistic than others of his breed, maybe no less, but not the sort to peg down a man's mind and turn loose a ravenous horde of worry ants on it. His own canteen was empty, and Suarez had already given him a drink from his twice.

He was hard to figure. Bert saw one thing in his favor, however: Howland's silver. Suarez didn't have the remotest idea of its whereabouts. Howland *could* have drawn a map, *could* have kept it on his person in a hollow heel, though it was highly unlikely he'd change boots and leave the map behind. Nobody in his right mind would do such a foolish thing. Suarez *knew* Howland; knew he was careful, buttoned up.

Suarez looked to Bert at the moment to be more confused than angry. Still, in the end he *would* shoot him, he reminded himself. Suarez wasn't stupid. In time he'd decide that if Bert actually knew the silver's whereabouts or if a map existed and he knew where it was, he'd have told him by now to save his skin.

Or could it be that Suarez had an altogether different reason for delaying his execution? Did his instincts warn him that the law was closing in and that if it came to a showdown a hostage might come in handy, as had the old man at the mortuary? Could that be his reason for keeping him alive? He wished he knew, though if he did, he just might change Suarez's thinking if he talked too much about it.

"Tell ya what I'll do, Perforia..."

"Porfirio!"

"Whatever. I know my talkin' 'noys ya, and I do sometimes have a ten'cy to run off at the mouth, so maybe I'd best shut up. But there's one last thing 'fore I do. The bald fact is that I find all this terrible frustratin', knowin' sure as I know my name that that map is back there just waitin' for somebody to come along and find it, reco'nize what it's the map to, and go out and dig up all that pretty silver. The cops, the army, maybe some o' your competin' *compadres* ridin' by, stoppin', nosin' 'round.

"Tell ya 'nother place he coulda hid it: his derby hatband. He wasn't wearin' it when they pulled the Nombre de Dios job, right? They were all disguised as peons, 'member? He left his derby and his reg'lar duds back at the shack. That map could be inside the linin'. I 'member a hard case by the name o' Luther Mitchell stole a chest fulla Spanish doubloons with King Philip himself's face on 'em, curly wig and all, from the Wells Fargo depot in Laredo—"

Out snaked Suarez's right gun blasting, blowing Bert's hat off.

"One more word, I keel you! One! Say it! Speak!" Bert said nothing. "I theenk I keel you, anyway. I am seeck of having you around."

"*Jefe*..." Still holding his gun on Bert, Suarez turned his head. Two men were pointing southward. "*Caballaria!*"

• • • •

Suarez cursed, waved his gun sharply at Bert, ordering him ahead, and, when he did so, rode off after him. For the past half hour the terrain had become gradually and noticeably less rugged as they neared the area surrounding Lake de Santiaguillo. Quickly now, the speed, strength, and endurance of the troopers' grain-fed mounts over the outlaws' grass-fed ones began to tell. The troop began closing the less-than-a-mile gap separating them from their quarry. Suarez and Bert rode in the middle of the pack; seeing their pursuers begin to catch up, the men started to peel off, ignoring Suarez's bellow. The horse soldiers held the winning card of discipline, thought Bert. The outlaws realized it and were dropping out, every man for himself. Within seconds only three men remained close to Suarez and him.

The lake came into view, broad, holding barely a third of normal capacity, its surface glassy and stagnant-looking. To the right a ridge of hills rose sharply. Bert threw a glance behind them. Through the dust he could see the captain leading the charge, his saber out and pointing straight ahead, the guidon flapping, fit to rip free of its pole, a cloud of dust rising in the wake of the troop, dun-coloring the pale blue sky and obscuring the sun. He saw something else: The captain was an experienced chaser. He, too, saw the potential cover of the ridge and had shifted the point of his saber toward it. He obviously intended to get around it or up into it and thereby neutralize it as a hideaway for his quarry.

The troopers were spreading out, but unlike the outlaws, they did so in orderly fashion, keeping a proper distance between them, synchronizing perfectly. On the run at full gallop, they were still able to free their rifles from under their cantles, ready them and open fire. The first volley dropped two of the men still holding formation with Suarez and Bert. One, barely four feet to Bert's right, was hit in the neck, yelled, threw up his hands, and fell back over his horse's rump. The other was hit between the shoulder blades and died screaming accompaniment to his companion. Bert swallowed painfully hard, held his breath, and hunched lower in the saddle.

He shot a look to his right. Four troopers had sprinted ahead on the right flank and were now paralleling them. Were they to continue in the same direction, they would come up on the other side of the hills. Suarez took no notice of them. The sight of the ridge appeared to ease his anxiety, even to cheer him. He had to know them, reflected Bert. Perhaps they were trickier than they looked from the outside; perhaps once they got up into them they would elude their pursuers easily.

"Ride, *gringo*," rasped Suarez, "like you never ride before."

"I'm ridin', I'm ridin' . . ." Bert reassured him.

"Faster!"

Lead whined about their ears. Bert imagined one slug after another smashing into the small of his back. He ducked and ducked.

"We'll never make those hills."

"We weel, and when we do, we're reed of them. I know them like my face; they are so treecky, you could not track a lame cow among them. You'll see. . . ."

Bert grunted. The lone survivor of the three men who had stuck with them screamed, slumped forward, and tumbled to the side, striking the ground, his head smashing against a rock and crushing like a ripe melon.

"Fasterrrr!" bawled Suarez.

They had almost reached the hills. As if sensing that they were about to lose them, the troopers doubled their firepower, pouring a fierce volley at their backs. Where the other outlaws had gotten to by now Bert could only guess, but from what he could see he and Suarez were the only survivors.

They reached the hills and rushed up into them, hurtling to the top.

"Left, left, left!" burst Suarez.

Bert cut left down a narrow, twisting trail. The firing behind had stopped abruptly; all he could hear was the distant, muffled sound of hooves. Suarez barked and barked again, turning him left, right, right again, around a hill, up another, down into a yawning crevass to a clump of bushes at the bottom.

"Pull up, pull up, pull up!"

"I'm pullin', I'm pullin'!"

"Deesmount, hurry!"

They quickly got their horses behind the bushes. There was a cave. The dead embers of an old cook fire littered the ground at the mouth. There were scattered hoofprints. The stale air issuing from the cave carried the stink of a dead animal. Bert made a face.

"You don't like theese place? I do. They can look for hours, for days and never find eet, and best of all, there ees a secret way out to within sight of the San Juan del Rio road."

"Do me a favor, show me—"

"Ha!"

"I'm ser'ous. Whattaya want with me, for cripes' sake, I mean, really? You can run twice as far, twice as fast, alone."

"*Si.*" He leered. "Aren't you curious to know why I have let you leeve this long?"

"'Cause you know I know where the map is." Bert tapped his temple and returned the leer. "Which is in here, and you're not 'bout to kill the goose that could lay you the silver egg, right?"

"Wrong. You know notheeng. On, I admeet I was wrong in the beginning, when I said you were rideeng with Herbeert and you had a fight, and he left you tied. No, he took you preesoner because there was sometheeng you had he wanted. Notheeng to do with the silver. I remember you said he was holding you for ransom."

"I—"

"You started to tell me. I didn't believe you then, but tell me about eet. You work for Wells Fargo."

"Listen to me, there's ten thousand bucks in ransom waitin' in the big bank in Durango—"

"Liar!"

Death In Durango

"It's the bald truth!"

"Eet's a lie! Like all your other lies! Let me tell you how I see eet, how eet ees. Herbeert captured you to hold for ransom, that could be, *si*. But when he contacted your superiors askeeng for money, they turned heem down flat."

"They didn't! Check the bank, why don'tcha, you'll see whether I'm lyin' or not."

"All you do ees lie, every word out of your mouth. I should believe thees? What do you theenk I am, an eembecile?"

"Ten thousand dollars!"

"Listen to you, look at you, who would pay ten dollars for you, let alone such a sum? Ees your family wealthy? Does theese Wells Fargo throw eets money at *bandidos*?"

"At Howland. To ransom me, the best detective they got!"

"Ha, I have seen you in action; eef you are the best, I would hate to see the worst."

He shoved the muzzles of both his guns into Bert's midsection.

"I don't know what Herbeert had in mind for you. To settle an old score, perhaps? Is that eet? To hold you for ransom ees the last theeng, now I theenk about it. *Gringo*, you have told your last lie. Get down on your knees and say your prayers, then I weel shoot you. Kneel."

"You're makin' the biggest mistake o' your life."

Suarez cocked both guns. "You don't want to pray, okay."

His eyes dark with fury, his jaw muscles taut to snapping, he stepped back. Two shots rang. Bert half gasped. Suarez stood immobile, then slowly he lowered his guns. Down with them came his jaw; amazement spread over his face. He tried to speak. He gurgled, he dropped his guns, he fell dead.

"You okay?" called a voice behind Bert.

Bert steeled himself, then slowly turned his head and looked upward.

"Aw, for cripes' sakes..."

Leaving his horse, Ben came down, rattling pebbles and small stones down before him.

"What the devil—" started Bert.

"I followed the troop," Ben interrupted, "I moved off their right flank about a mile from the post. When I spotted you and your friends and saw these hills, I figured you'd cut for them. I got up here even before the shooting started. I was up top and watched you two ride all the way around Robin Hood's barn to this place."

He shoved his gun in his belt.

"What the devil you doin' in Mexico?" Bert demanded.

"Saving your life, it looks like. Don't start, Bert, you really didn't think I'd sit on my haunches and wait till God knows when for word that Cutler finally got you."

"That'll be the day."

Ben eyed Suarez's prostrate body. "Aren't you even going to thank me for saving your life?"

"Big deal. I'd like to thank you for not stickin' your big nose into my bus'ness, that I'd really like, but I can't do it can I?"

"You're incorrigible."

"You got no bus'ness comin' all the way down here. Look atcha, you're not even back together again, pasty as a sheet, worn down to a nub..."

"And you look marvelous. Satisfy my curiosity. What, if anything, have you accomplished since you've been down here? I mean, besides getting yourself captured by the locals, held for ransom, arrested, jailed, captured a second time... Is there more?"

"Oh, shut up."

"It might interest you to know that while you've been cavorting about between the frying pan and the fire, I've made a good deal of progress in what you came down here to do. For one thing, I've found Cutler."

"He's in Durango, I know that. Tell me somethin' I don't know."

"What's he disguised as?"

"Just a plain ol' disguise, nothin' fancy."

"You haven't the slightest idea. He's a priest with a beard and an eye patch."

"I know, I know."

"Why don't you sit down before you fall down? It's a long story."

"So you found the one-eyed scum. Big deal. Who asked you to? Not me. I oughta bust your face, disobeyin' me, runnin' down here, raisin' hell nobody asked you to, interferin'. When you gonna learn!"

On he raved; Ben let him. Let him get it out of his system, he thought wearily. Let the fires of his irritation die, give his ego a few minutes to recover from the bruising. He could tell by his face and his tone that that was what it was. He'd stepped on his tender toes, and nothing would serve but for Bert to take time out to hand Ben's head to him. No man can be grateful when his son outdoes him. When he winds up saving his life in the bargain, ingratitude can easily degenerate into disgust, even loathing.

Bert finally talked himself out, but from the look on his face his bitterness had not ebbed even slightly. Ben saw only one course open to him: Back away and let him take over the reins; let him give the orders and call the shots from here on. Offer no suggestions unless they were asked for, which they wouldn't be.

"Okay," he said mildly, "what do we do now?"

"*We* don't do anythin'; *I* get back to workin' on what I come down here to do, which I don't have to go into with the likes o' you."

"You want me to turn around and go back to San Francisco?"

"Ya can go to blazes for all I care, just stay outta my hair."

"And what will you do, go scour the city looking for him? How many priests with beards will you call out and maybe wound, even kill, before you get the right one?"

"The right one's wearin' a eye patch; how many priests built like him with beards wear eye patches?"

"You're right."

"Boy, that kinda figgerin' could be a real big help to me. I'm missin' the boat for fair, not pullin' you up on the wagon."

"Must you be sarcastic? There's an easier way to find him if you're interested. The woman I mentioned, Mrs. O'Rourke—"

"I'm not interested," Bert interrupted. "Ringin' her in'd only tangle things up. Too many cooks spoil the soup, ya know. Ya should."

He paused and glanced about. "I gotta go. By myself if ya don't mind, or even if ya do." He looked down at Suarez. "So long, Perforia."

Sixteen

Not a single trooper could be seen when Bert came down out of the hills. Ben followed him out. Bert started off toward Durango but had not ridden a quarter of a mile before he pulled his horse to a stop. He turned and waited for Ben. The scowl had deserted his face, Ben noted, coming closer. Had he had a change of heart toward him?

"Hi, son..."

No change of heart, decided Ben, he wanted something.

"What's the matter?"

"Nothin's the matter. Only a small, little item I seemed to have overlooked in all the hul'baloo. The bald truth is, all this runnin' 'round has tapped me out. Howland took what was left in my wallet. Before ya head north, wouldja mind lendin' me a few bucks? I promise I'll pay ya back outta my next paycheck."

"You quit the company."

"I don't mean from Wells Fargo, I mean the railroad. I

been thinking' ser'ous o' tyin' up with the Union Pacific or maybe the Great Northern.''

"Oh, stop it!"

"Are ya gonna lend me a hunnerd bucks or not?"

"What do you need with money? Any expenses come along, I'll see to them. I brought plenty with me; we can live comfortably for the next four weeks if this takes that long."

"I'm talkin' *me*, not *we*...."

"Give it up, Bert. You're broke, you haven't enough for your next drink, let alone a hotel room, meals, a gun. I'll take care of everything; as long as we're partners, why shouldn't I?"

"That's blackmail!"

"Blackmail? How do you figure? I offer to meet every possible expense."

"Ya oughta be 'shamed. All right, all right, all right, I'll letcha tag along."

"Will you really?"

"Shut up. Just don't go stickin' your oar in every which way. I'm callin' the shots, you follow orders. Or else."

"Of course. I wouldn't have it any other way."

"Plain blackmail, extortionin' a man when he's temp'rary down on the balls o' his heels. Shame on ya!"

• • • •

At Ben's suggestion on reaching Durango they split up to search for Cutler. The plan was to rendezvous in the lobby of the Victoria at eight sharp. But they returned from their respective searches wearing identical expressions of defeat. Bert asked at the desk for a room; he was told that the hotel was filled at the moment. Arrangements were made for a cot to be brought up to Ben's room.

"Ya gimme your bed and you can use the cot. Cots are great for the back, ya know, good and firm," Bert said firmly, knowingly.

"Never mind. This prowling about trying to keep out of his sight if we do bump into him is ridiculous."

"He's prob'ly beat it; he's sure had time 'nough to."

"I don't think so."

They sat in overstuffed chairs, Bert working over a mouthful of a Mexican brand of chewing tobacco with the impressive name of Chihuahua Campeon, complaining between chews that it was too fruity and too soft, while Ben tugged thoughtfully on his last Jersey cheroot.

"Ya don't know..."

"The more I think about it, the more *she* looks like the key. Think about it. She's the reason he came down here. Whatever it is they're cooking up requires them to get together. Probably periodically."

"You don't know if they're cookin' up anythin'. You're just guessin'."

"Common sense says they must be. I know enough to corroborate it—in my opinion I do. She lied to me about her husband, so he probably wasn't the only thing she lied about. She talked my ear off for five days but never once mentioned Portland, apart from that was where she was coming from. She probably never went near there. She never did say what she was doing if she did...."

"You said visitin' her sister-in-law."

"Why should I believe that?"

"Why shouldn' ya? Sounds straight to me. Rel'tives visit each other all the time. There doesn' have to be some deep, dark secret plan to bring 'em together." Bert sighed. "I can see the handwritin' on the wall. You're determined to ring her into this."

"I'd say she's already in. Don't you understand, she's our only link to him down here. She knows where he's staying, and probably his comings and goings as well."

"And you plan to knock on her door and ask her, and she's gonna tell ya all 'bout it. Ev'rythin'."

"I'd hardly ask her directly. Look, I can either trick her into divulging what she knows about him or keep an eye on her, follow her every step away from home, and sooner or later she'll have to meet him again."

"She doesn' have to do anythin'."

"She's our only hope."

"I dis'gree. We only been lookin' four hours. I say we give it at least two or three more days."

"Why waste the time? Tell you what. First thing tomorrow I'll go over to her place in Independence Square—I've got the address—and see her. She offered to be my guide; she suggested we take in the bullfights. She won't see anything suspicious in my wanting to spend a few hours with her, and in those few hours I'll get her to open up about him."

"How?"

"I'll..."

"Yeah?"

"I'll tell her straight out that I saw her talking to a priest and that I recognized him."

"He's disguised, 'member? How do you rec'nize somebody when they're all gussied up to look different from what they are? B'sides, you think she doesn't know him for what he is, a rotten scum murderin' thief wanted all over the West and prob'bly even down here? If she knows that, she knows you gotta be up to no good askin' after him. So what's she gonna do, hand him to ya on a silver platter or tip him off you're lookin' for him? Benjamin, you are such a wishful thinker, you and your common sense just don't make sense."

"I'm still going to call on her."

"You do that, and give her my best regards. Meantime, I'll keep lookin'."

"I wish you wouldn't..."

"Not 'thout you, right? Ya still think I can't take him 'thout ya, that it?"

"Can't we please try just this phase of it my way? Just try..."

"You. Me, I'm keepin' after the fox's tail."

Ben sighed and puffed on his cheroot. "Just see that you don't go wandering out of town, especially in the direction of Nombre de Dios. They're no doubt still looking for you."

"Baloney."

A familiar figure filled the doorway, a willowy, lovely, dark-eyed girl about seventeen on his arm. Captain Sidonia looked significantly less impressive out of uniform. He waved to Ben.

"Mr. Slaughter, may I present my daughter, Consuela. My dear, Mr. Benjamin Slaughter, and ahhhh, it is your father!"

Ben introduced Bert, studying Sidonia's eyes as he did so. They didn't narrow, nor did they appear to harden; still, it was difficult to tell what was going on in the mind behind them.

"It is such a lovely evening, Consuela and I decided we would take a longer constitutional than usual. I hoped I might find you here, Ben. Word came in late this afternoon of the action between Suarez and Captain Frasquita and his men over by the lake. The outlaws were wiped out, except for Suarez; he got away as usual."

"He's dead," said Ben flatly, startling the girl and raising Sidonia's left eyebrow. "I shot him."

"You followed the troop out there when Frasquita denied your request to accompany them. I was sure you would."

Ben told him about the incident near the cave, stressing the fact that if he hadn't killed the outlaw, Suarez would have killed Bert. Sidonia turned to Bert, smiling a trifle coldly, Ben noted.

"So now you are back here looking for..." He looked at Ben. "What was his name?"

"Cutler," mumbled Ben.

"Yes. Mr. Slaughter, your vendetta with this man is no concern of mine, nor do I wish to make it my business, but I ask you to keep in mind that Durango is not Tombstone, Arizona. We do not permit strangers to shoot it out in the middle of main street at high noon. I personally could not care less what you do to each other, just don't do it in Durango."

"Captain—" began Bert.

Up came Sidonia's hand. "You recently broke jail in Nombre de Dios. I could arrest you and hold you for Chief Flores, but with Suarez dead, there would be no way to prove your innocence, and even though I am not in possession of all the facts, I believe you are. But in this tense climate, innocent though you are, it could go hard for you if you are recaptured. Your wisest course would be to get out of the state as soon as possible."

Bert nodded. While the captain was addressing him he had not taken his scowl off Ben. He continued to immolate him with his eyes. Sidonia and Consuela wished the two of them a good evening and left.

"These badges stick together like Diamond Liquid glue, mends anythin' strong as a rock...."

Ben scoffed. "You weren't listening. He just let you off the hook."

"You hadda tell him 'bout Cutler, didn't ya; ya couldn't keep your big yap shut. Why'ntcha get one o' those big fat auctioneer meg'phones and get up on the balcony and tell the whole world, for cripes' sakes!"

"Will you quiet down! Stop making a spectacle!" Ben then lowered his tone. "I had to level with him. I could hardly lie when he asked me what you were doing down here. He's a decent man, he's fair; he's willing to keep what he knows in confidence. He doesn't have to, but he's doing it. The least we can do is get out."

"You get out, I'm gonna find that scum if I got to root here the next six years!"

He spat his chaw at a nearby spittoon, missing the hole, splattering the edge, and stalking off.

"Where are you going?"

"What does it look like? To bed. And when you come up, see that ya don't go makin' a big racket settin' your cot up."

Seventeen

Bert insisted on accompanying Ben to number 113 Independence Square the next morning.

"You should have stayed at the hotel," said Ben as they stood before Bridget O'Rourke's door. The lion-face knocker glared uninvitingly at his upraised hand.

"And do what, look for cockroaches?"

"You hard Captain Sidonia..."

"Wouldja b'lieve I don't care?"

He reached past Ben and rapped the knocker too loudly. The door opened revealing the maid, her face seamed with age, her hair bound too tightly under her little cap. She studied them with a stern, suspicious expression. Ben doffed his hat and elbowed Bert to do the same.

"Good morning, Benjamin and Egbert Slaughter to see Mrs. O'Rourke."

"My mistress is not at home."

"Oh?" said Ben, "she went out early?"

"Early yesterday. She has gone to Mexico City."

Father and son exchanged glances.

"Ahhh," said Ben, "of course. I completely forgot she told me she was going."

He could feel Bert's eyes drilling him. He was standing to his left and slightly behind him so he couldn't see his face, but he was sure it bore the expression of disgust Bert usually reserved for his son's lame efforts at lying. Ben was fleetingly tempted to step aside and tell him to take over.

"When she comin' back?" Bert asked pointedly.

"Not till after the holiday, señor."

"Holiday?"

"Independence Day. September sixteenth."

"Oh. What's today?" he asked Ben.

"The twelfth," said the maid.

"Did she go by train?" Ben asked.

"*Si*, the eight-thirty. It makes many stops and is a long journey, I believe more than six hundred miles."

"And did she go alone?"

"With him."

"Her friend, Father..."

"Fitzgerald."

"With the beard and the eye patch."

"*Si*. He picked her up in a buggy."

"Thank you very much," he said.

"You are welcome. Do you wish to leave your card?"

"No, no, we'll be around when she gets back."

"Very well."

She closed the door in their faces. They stood staring at the lion knocker.

"What the devil..." began Bert.

"What does she want in Mexico City?"

"Who cares what she wants? He's with her, he's all that matters. Looks like your friend Captain Sidonia's gonna get his wish. Let's go back to that fleabag hotel, pack up, and catch the first train south."

"They've got a twenty-four-hour head start; they must have arrived sometime last night." Ben rubbed his chin and thoughtfully stared a hundred miles away. "Independence Day... What the devil is going on?"

"They'll be havin' a big cel'bration, bands and dancin', fireworks, speeches."

"And Bridget O'Rourke and Father Fitzgerald."

"C'mon..."

"Wait." Ben rapped on the door again.

"What now?"

"Mexico City's big, Bert, we'll find her a lot easier if we show her picture around. She must have a small photograph."

"What makes you think the maid'll give it to—"

The door opened; the woman eyed them questioningly.

"Sorry to bother you again," said Ben pleasantly. "I just remembered, I carelessly left my wallet in the restaurant the other night when Mrs. O'Rourke and I had dinner. I left before she did. She left word at my hotel that she brought it home for me. It's in her night-table drawer."

"She did not say anything to me."

"I'm sure you'll find it in the drawer."

"One moment."

She left the door ajar. They waited until she reached the top of the stairs before going in. The front room was spacious and tastefully decorated, creating a light and airy ambience. They looked around. A large portrait of Bridget smiled down from above the fireplace. Bert spotted a small framed oval photograph of husband and wife on the sideboard. Sean O'Rourke looked remarkably studious for a revolutionary. Ben snatched up the picture, jammed it in his belt, and buttoned all three buttons of his jacket. Bert started for the door. Ben grabbed his arm.

"Wait..."

They heard a door close upstairs. The maid was humming to herself.

"I'll go and unlock the back door. You get her to the front, outside if you can. Yes, by all means get her outside. Give me five minutes; I want to look around upstairs."

Footsteps sounded above.

"What for?"

"Just do it."

"What'll I talk to her 'bout?"

"Use your imagination; just keep her outside. Sssh..."

He ran back to the kitchen, unlocked the door, and returned just as the maid's skirt appeared descending the stairs. Down she came, shaking her head.

"It is not in the night-table drawer."

"Ahhh, she must have changed her mind and put it someplace else," said Ben. "Don't bother looking around, I'll be seeing her when she gets back." He turned to Bert. "I'd better get right over to police headquarters."

"Yeah. Wait for me there," his father agreed.

Ben thanked the maid and went out, the flat of his hand pressed against the framed photograph in his belt. Reaching the sidewalk, he ran down the street and around the corner.

"Police?" asked the maid.

"Señora . . ." Bert started.

"Señorita."

"Whatever. I got to level with ya; maybe you'd best step outside so ya can get plenty o' fresh air, so's ya won't pass out."

"Pass out?"

He eased her outside, closing the door to within an inch of the jamb. He flashed his ID card so fast, she couldn't possibly read it. "My son and I are both international detectives. We're on the trail o' that bogus priest calls himself Father Fitzgerald."

Her eyes saucered. "He is not a real priest?"

Bert shook his head, his expression grim. "It's one o' his fav'rite disguises. Brace yourself. His real name's Herbert Howland, better known to the newspapers and the police as the Tombstone Strangler."

"What is strang-lar?"

He gripped his throat with both hands and stuck out his tongue as far as it would go. She recoiled in horror.

"Estrangular!"

"Right. He's strangled twelve, maybe fifteen women all over. He usu'ly strikes up a 'quaintance with 'em, gets to know 'em real good, gets 'em to draw all their money outta the bank, then go onna trip with him, to get 'em away from people that know 'em and in 'mong strangers, ya know?

Death In Durango   125

Then he strangles 'em and takes all their money." Again he gripped his throat.

"No!"

"Yeah. He's a bad customer, the worst. Wanted in ten states and twelve or fifteen terr'tories. My partner and I almost caught up with him here in Durango. Now we'll have to follow him down there."

• • • •

A six-foot solid plank fence enclosed the backyard, but there was a door with a simple thumb latch. Ben got inside the house, tiptoeing through the kitchen into the front room and up the carpeted stairs. Bridget's bedroom was located at the corner of the house, giving her double windows in two walls. He went straight to her vanity and began rummaging through the drawers.

• • • •

"I only hope we catch up with 'em b'fore he busts her neck."

"Merciful God!"

"Take a good deep breath, thatta girl."

"Perhaps you are mistaken. Perhaps he is not the one you are after—"

"Not a chance. Father Fitzgerald's one o' his fav'rite aliases." He went on to describe Cutler in detail. "That's him, right?"

"It sounds like him. I can't be certain. I only saw him once. Through the front window seated at the reins of the buggy when he came to drive them to the station. *Madre de Dios*, this is horrible! My poor mistress!"

"I'm sorry to have to be the bearer o' such rotten, vicious news, but don't give up hope. Light some candles and pray she'll be all right, that she won't be victim number sixteen."

"She cannot be! God is merciful. He will not let him strike down one so young, so beautiful, so good. Poor mistress . . ."

"Take it easy. He knows we're after him. Maybe he'll play it safe this time out and hold off. Well, I'll say good-bye, I gotta get over to headquarters and hook up with my partner and see if any more news has come in on him. Don't worry, worryin's not gonna save her life. Just try to relax; it's a great day, warm, sunny, the birds singin' their guts out. Relax and enjoy it. And wish us luck."

He touched the brim of his hat. She continued to stare fearfully as he descended the steps and started up the street in the direction Ben had taken five minutes before. He saluted a nursemaid pushing a baby carriage. When he got to the corner, he turned and looked back. The maid had gone inside, closing the door. He turned the corner. Halfway down the block Ben appeared, emerging from an alley. Under his arm was a book.

"What's that?"

"Lucky for us the lady's a save-all. Have a look."

It was a scrapbook. In it were newspaper photos, drawings, and items concerning one man exclusively.

Ben's face reflected triumph. "Porfirio Diaz!"

"Who's he?"

Ben's eyes gleamed. "Ssssh, I get it. I get it! That's it! Of course!"

"Whattaya talkin' about?"

"Don't you see? Can't you put it together?" Bert had closed the scrapbook. He tapped it and bussed it fondly. "This cinches it. Bridget O'Rourke is carrying on her dead husband's campaign to overthrow the government. It's what he wanted, it's what he died wanting. Nobody was good enough to step into Benito Juarez's shoes, least of all President Sebastian Lerdo de Tejada. So what has she decided? To remove Lerdo and replace him with her hero."

"Diaz."

"She's hired Cutler to assassinate Lerdo."

"You're kiddin'..."

"Bert, what else would she hire him for? What is he best at? And why the disguise? And why have they run off to Mexico City? Independence Day, that's why. You said it before, a huge celebration, bands, dancing, fireworks, speeches. And when President Lerdo stands up to make his speech, the assassin will strike. That's her plan. Bet your life on it!"

"Lemme see that book."

Bert leafed through it. Page after page, Diaz popped into view: in the dress uniform of a general, complete with epaulets, high collar covered with gold braid, gold braid across his chest and down his lapels, and gleaming metals; short, dark hair; mustache and straggly goatee. Another picture displayed three times the number of medals, his hair longer and parted on the left side. And photographs of him in civilian clothes, one dated only two months earlier. His mustache had thickened, now all but obscuring his mouth. His goatee had become a beard, and his dark eyes smoldered with ambition.

But it was the photograph on the last page that confirmed Ben's assertion. It was not of Diaz but of President Lerdo. A large red *X* and the single word, *muerte*, verified Bridget's plan for him.

"We gotta get down there pronto," said Bert.

"Relax, a dollar to a dime says he won't strike until the big day."

"We gotta find 'em when we get there."

"We will. Let's go check the train schedule at the station. And before we leave, I must send a wire to James Hume."

"What for?"

"I promised I'd stay in touch. Besides, he should know you're safe so he can cancel the letter of credit or whatever it is at the bank, the ransom money."

"Tell ya what, ya go wire him, I'll go to the bank and pick up that money; we're gonna need it. Not all o' it, just some."

"Forget it, Bert."

"It's my money!"

"It's Wells Fargo's. I said forget it!"

"All right, all right, all right..."

Eighteen

A tear rolled slowly down Ben's cheek and plopped to rest on the back of his hand capping his knee. His father had his arm around him, trying to console him. No easy job; how does one console an eight-year-old whose dog has been run over by a freight wagon only an hour before?

Ben sniffled and fought back more tears. " 'S not fair!"

"Life's not, son. How many times I tol'ja that?"

"Albert was just a puppy."

"Goin' on six. He liked to chase cats. If he didn't, he wouldn't'a chased that tom under the wagon. Wasn't the driver's fault."

"I didn't say it was!"

"Easy, Ben...."

"Why couldn't he just get hurt a little instead of killed? If he broke his leg, it could heal. I'd take care of him till he was right again. Oh, Paw, I miss him so much. I loved him so!"

He threw himself against Bert's chest, sobbing his heart

out. Bert patted him gently and said nothing. They had just come from burying Albert in the backyard. He looked out the window. He could see the little mound and the cross Ben had fashioned under the apple tree. The day was appropriately dismal, threatening rain. It was a harsh world, he thought, that takes a little boy's dog from him so abruptly, so cruelly. Ben continued sobbing quietly. He'd have to look around, Bert thought, get him another dog as soon as he could. A pup barely out of weaning, a really cute one with ears too big for its head, rubbery legs, and a tail that never stopped wagging; one that liked to lick little boys' faces. One that needed a friend as much as Ben did at the moment. But really cute; it would have to be to win over Ben's heart, drive out his sadness.

He brought the puppy home the next day after work. It was no bigger than a minute with a little pink nose, ears too long, a tight little bundle of energy. When he walked in the door, Ben was sitting at the back window, looking out at Albert's grave. He wasn't crying, he was cried out, but Bert had never seen him looking so sad. Except for when he stopped crying after his mother died the year before. Ben turned in his chair when he heard him come in. Bert cradled the puppy in his forearm.

"Vis'tor to see ya, Ben."

"I don't care. Don't want to see him. Take him away, please?"

"You don't mean that."

"I do, cross my heart I do. I can't stand the sight of him."

"He likes lookin' at you. Give him a chance, Ben."

"No!"

"Give him just five minutes to, you know, get 'quainted. Look at him, he's as cute as a button. Look at that tongue, must be six inches long. He's just a baby...."

"I don't care."

Ben averted his eyes, determined not to look. Bert walked over to him, stroking the puppy's head.

"He wants to make friends."

"I don't care. Please!"

He got up.

"Where ya goin'?"

"To my room. I just want to be alone."

He was looking at the puppy for the first time. Sensing attention, it began to wag its tail.

"Look at him, he's sayin' hello!"

"He's just waggin' his tail, that's all. He's runty. All wet around the nose. Probably got fleas."

"He's real soft when you pet him. Warm. Friendly little cuss. Hey, I got to go down to Rathbone's for a loaf o' bread and Jamoka and such. I'll just leave him here on the sofa till I get back. Okay?"

"I don't care. I'm going upstairs."

He had moved only two steps from his chair. His eyes were now glued to the puppy. Bert set it on the sofa.

"Be right back."

He went out, closing the door. He stood a moment, cocking an ear and listening intently but could hear nothing inside. He walked down the side of the house to the rear and sneaked a look through the window. Ben was standing where he'd left him. The puppy had found a home on the sofa, rolling around playfully, stopping, staring at Ben, who was staring at it, the puppy panting, its tongue unfurled and waggling, then going back to rolling around. Bert couldn't see Ben's face until he turned and started for the stairs. The puppy jumped off the sofa and followed, wagging its tail relentlessly. Ben stopped.

"Stop following me. Go away!"

His words had no effect. When he turned and resumed walking toward the stairs, it followed. Again he turned and upbraided it. It paid no attention; it wanted to play. It yipped and bounced on its forepaws and wagged its tail furiously.

"Awwww," growled Ben, scowling.

Bert watched him. As he stood looking down at it, Ben's face began to soften. He was almost smiling when he bent and picked it up and cradled it in his arms. When it licked him, he beamed. Bert went back around front and started off for Rathbone's.

Albert Two lived until Ben's third year of college. That

winter it caught a cold that developed into pneumonia. It died the last day of January. When Ben came home for spring vacation, Bert told him the bad news. He took it philosophically. It was, after all, a tragedy more easily tolerated at twenty than at eight.

• • • •

The mountains of the State of Zacatecas sprawled about like a great herd of sleepy woolly mammoths, though the capital city of that name, located more than a hundred miles southeast of Durango, nestled in the slopes of a mountain called Cerro de la Bufa because it resembled a *bufa*, a Spanish wineskin. The railroad followed the course of least obstruction, zigzagging, meandering, and all but completely encircling the more formidable peaks. It was a tedious journey but, unlike the ride down through the desert, pleasantly cool. Every car was jammed with passengers and their luggage, the majority bound for Mexico City and the pending holiday festivities. Endless babbling, shouting children, and laughter made it impossible for Ben to sleep. Bert had no such problem; he slouched, his head against the window post, his hat over his face, snoring lustily. But when the train jerked to a sudden stop before slowly proceeding, it woke him.

"I meant to ask you," said Ben, "what did you say to the maid to keep her outside the front door? It certainly worked."

"It couldn't miss."

"What?"

"I told her ya were crazy."

"You did not!"

"Cross my heart. Told her ya just 'magined ya left your wallet at the restaurant, 'magined ya had dinner with her nibs. Told her the doctor said it was very 'portant I humor ya, otherwise ya'd go wild, that it all come from a terrible bump on your head. Ya 'magine you're a great detective and I humor ya into lettin' ya think so, lettin' ya tag along and question folks and such. Told her how grateful I was for her playin' along with ya, 'pologized for imposin' and takin' her time and all. She was real sympathetic, said she had a cousin was the same way, same 'fliction, and said she hoped ya'd get cured someday; I told her the doctors were workin' on it."

"Get serious for a minute," Ben said. "I've been thinking, this is a very big kettle of fish we're getting into. We're foreigners, neither of us speaks the language, we don't know the customs, the rules, the laws, and here we are on the way to the capital to foil an attempt to assassinate the president. Bert, I think the smartest thing we can do is go straight to the American Embassy as soon as we arrive and lay all our cards on the table."

"I think that's the dumbest thing we can do."

"Why?"

"Number one, the whole thing's so harebrained, the ambass'dor likely won't b'lieve a word of it; number two, even if he does, he won't lift a finger to help."

"Why wouldn't he?"

"It's none o' his bus'ness, that's why, none o' the U.S.'s. No, I say we get off the train down there, go lookin' for Mr. Scum, corner him, and punch his ticket. Then get out. I don't mind missin' the fireworks."

"Shoot him in cold blood."

"Ya object to that? He shot you in cold blood, didn't he? Tried his best to kill ya."

"I say corner him, capture him, and take him back to San Francisco."

"Like a satchel fulla souvenirs. No thanks."

"You've just got to do it your way."

"It's not mine, I didn't invent it. It's eye for a eye."

"You'd lower yourself."

"I won't be lowerin' nothin', just givin' him what he deserves, fin'ly, at long last." He was studying Ben, his expression disapproving. "What ails you, anyhow? Ya goin' chickenhearted on me? I notice ya didn't have any trouble gunning down Suarez."

"That's different, he was just about to kill you."

"'Sno different. Lemme tell ya somethin, point up how

wrong ya are. Let's say back in Frisco, when he stepped outta that alley and shot at you, he killed ya. You're dead. No hospital, doctor, nothin', dead. I hear 'bout it, I go after him, find him, call him out, kill him. You see anything wrong in that?"

"I'm not dead."

Bert flung his hand. "I don't wanna discuss it. We head there, find him, kill him. I don't care 'bout the pres'dent, your lady friend, the ambass'dor, their big to-do Fourth o' July in September, nothin' but him. Today's Sunday, we'll get in early tomorrow mornin'. That gives me better'n three days. You go see the ambass'dor, you find her, you eat tacos and dance in the street, just count me out."

"You want to split up?"

"The second we set foot offa this thing. *Adios, amigo.* Next time you see me'll be back in Frisco. Or not. Wherever we meet, if ever, you'll see the biggest, beamin'est smile you've ever seen on this face!"

"The face of an obstinate jackass."

"Awwww..."

Again Bert flung his hand. He slumped in his corner against the window post, tilted his hat over his face, folded his arms, and resumed snoring. Ben grinned, sighed, leaned over, and tapped him awake. Bert lifted his hat and opened one eye.

"Aren't you forgetting something? If you're going off on your own, what do you intend to do for money? You're broke, remember?"

"Don't need money. I can sleep in a alley, I can pinch food. Even go 'thout. All I need is my gun and six cartridges, and them I got. Take your money and stick it in your ear for all I care."

Down dropped his hat and his eyelid; up came his snoring. It was getting dark out. Despite the persisting racket surrounding them—loud conversations, laughter, singing, occasional yelling, and the sounds of the train—despite his firm conviction that as tired as he was, he'd never be able to fall asleep, Ben did so. No sooner did he then Bert's eyes eased open. Up came his hat. He straightened slightly, reached over, and deftly plucked Ben's wallet from his inside pocket. He relieved it of fifty dollars, started to restore it, changed his mind, and took an additional ten spot. Then slid the wallet back into Ben's pocket.

Ben never felt a thing. Bert pocketed the money, closed his eyes, and went back to sleep.

Nineteen

Ben sat on the rosewood bench, the scrapbook in his lap, his hat set upon it. To his left at the end of the narrow corridor stood a grandfather clock ticking solemnly, deliberately goading his impatience. He had been passed through the gate by the two guards, American Marines in uniform, and greeted by a mincing male secretary who looked as if he'd risen from his coffin to do so.

Being made to wait didn't annoy him; it was, after all, only eight or nine minutes since he sat down. Bert annoyed him. It wasn't until he arrived at the embassy and went into his wallet to pay the driver that he discovered that sixty dollars was missing. They had parted company at the railroad station upon arriving. He had wondered at the time why Bert was so effusive in wishing him luck and so casual at leaving him, going off without a cent in his pockets.

"Now he can add pickpocketing to his list of talents."

He'd catch up with him later. Ambassador Henry Lane

Wilson came first. It was in his power to nip the whole scheme in the bud; if the Mexican government was alerted and took the necessary precautions, Cutler would be stopped before any damage was done. The clock chimed eleven. He yawned, scratched his side, and eased the sleep out of the corner of his right eye. He could hear steps. The secretary was coming back. He still looked like a cadaver, a man cut off in his prime, unwilling to accept his fate, walking around in defiance of it.

"Mr. Slaughter, the ambassador will see you now."

"Thank you."

He had gotten up at the man's approach. Someone was coming from the opposite direction. He turned the corner, took one look at Ben, stopped, gawked, and beamed.

"Ben Slaughter!"

"Mark Otterbourg! What the devil..."

They had been classmates at the University of Virginia, close friends graduating together. Marcus Otterbourg, Sr., had been the American consul in Mexico, preceding the appointment of Henry Lane Wilson as America's first ambassador to her southern neighbor. Mark looked like his father, prematurely paunchy, with reddish-blond hair that defied neatening by brush and comb surmounting pink-tinted good looks that were dominated by blue eyes that entranced practically every female they fell upon.

"Never mind me!" burst Mark. "What are *you* doing down here? I thought you went to work for Wells Fargo with your dad."

"I did, I am. We're down here chasing a suspect."

The secretary stood awkwardly shifting from one foot to the other, his face darkening. He quite obviously had other things to do. "Mr. Slaughter..."

"Mark, I've got to go in and talk to the ambassador. Matter of life and death, I'm afraid."

"Tell me after." He pointed down the way he had come. "My office is around the corner, second door on your right. I'll be waiting. We can have lunch."

"Great."

The sliding doors were opened for him. Ambassador Wilson was seated at his desk. He wore a thick pad of shining light hair parted on the left and a flowing soup-strainer mustache in the fashion of the day. His eyebrows were full and dark in contrast to his hair, lending much-needed sternness to his otherwise unimpressive brown eyes. He was a handsome man in his fifties, the kind who stood out at formal affairs, thought Ben, looking his handsomest, trim and fit among the bellied and aging Mexican politicians and generals. The secretary slid the doors closed. The American flag hung from the wall over the oriel window behind the ambassador. Gracing the other walls were framed photographs of American presidents and one, Ben noticed, of Marcus Otterbourg. President Grant's larger-than-lifesize likeness occupied the place of honor at the center of the wall to the right.

Ambassador Wilson extended his hand, and Ben shook it.

"Please have a chair. May I offer you a cigar?"

Ben declined, thanking him. He watched in silence as he lit one.

"What can I do for you?"

Ben detailed the situation, avoiding any mention of his and Bert's personal "interest" in apprehending Cutler. He chose his words ruefully, stressing the perilousness of the plot, avoiding the temptation to overdramatize. He offered the scrapbook to support his contention and noted in passing that Wells Fargo wanted Cutler for six separate robberies and two attempted murders. Wilson said nothing, not once interrupting him, but his eyes affirmed that he was paying close attention to his every word.

"The thing is, sir, if we wait until Thursday and President Lerdo's speech... I'm assuming he will speak."

"Oh, yes. Traditionally from the balcony overlooking Zócalo Plaza. He usually concludes his speech by striking the Independence bell, signaling the beginning of the festivities," the ambassador answered.

"He may not get to strike it. Nor even speak, for that matter."

"Yes, yes, yes." He seemed suddenly struck by impatience. "Mr. Slaughter, what you've told me certainly sounds genuine—that is, I'm sure your concern is. And it appears warranted. Let me explain something. We're here primarily to protect American interests and assist American nationals in any way we can. In these regards we're no different than our embassies in other countries. We are here at the sufferance of the Mexican government. Consequently we are necessarily limited in what we can do simply because we are on foreign soil. One rule we must scrupulously observe above all others: We must keep our noses out of Mexico's internal affairs. They're none of our business."

"I understand, sir, and I appreciate the necessity of it, but this is an unusual situation. We're talking about assassination."

"Possible assassination."

"Imminent assassination. Knowing Cutler and Mrs. O'Rourke, it's an absolute certainty. Look at the last page of that book; President Lerdo's picture crossed out, the word *death* scrawled across it."

"I saw it. I'm inclined to agree with you, but think about it a minute. What if there is no attempt? What if it turns out to be pure speculation on your part and nothing more? I alert His Excellency to the threat, other high officials, and Independence Day comes and goes and no attempt is made. To say I'd end up with a red face would be putting it mildly. I'd be crying wolf, scaring everybody out of their wits, then winding up having to apologize."

"Isn't that better than standing idly by and crossing our fingers so nothing'll happen?"

"Come, come, I don't mind being embarrassed, but that's not really the point."

"What is?"

"Precisely what I've been trying to tell you. We don't meddle in their internal affairs!"

"Mr. Ambassador, Cutler's an American. He's down here for one purpose only. If something isn't done to stop him, he'll assassinate the president. How will that make the

U.S. look? And God forbid word leaks out that we knew, that we could have taken action and didn't."

"Word leaks out? Are you threatening me?"

"No, sir."

"Mr. Slaughter, do this much for me. Leave the scrapbook with me; let me think about it. If you don't mind, I'd like to discuss it with others here at the embassy." He stood up, signaling an end to the interview. Again he offered his hand. "Come back tomorrow morning. We'll talk further."

"Yes. Thank you."

● ● ● ●

Bert was right. The ambassador wasn't interested in getting involved. Official reluctance to "meddle" in Mexico's internal affairs was a poor excuse for inaction but looked to be the only excuse he would get.

"Incredible..."

He turned the corner. Mark Otterbourg's door was closed. He knocked. Mark came out smiling.

"All done? How'd you make out?" He snickered. "What did you want, a loan so you can buy your ticket home? Hungry?"

"Same old Otterbourg, asks a dozen questions, never waits for a single answer. I skipped breakfast, I'm starved."

"There's a place two blocks from here. You look disgusted, what happened?"

Ben told him on the way to the restaurant, even to admitting his and Bert's personal involvement with Cutler, though denying that it had anything to do with the imminent assassination. He touched on the high points of the preceding few days. He knew Mark well, knew he would offer to help, even if it meant sticking his neck out.

"Did you get the impression that Henry believed what you told him?"

"He said he did, but he still won't do anything. He refuses to poke into Mexico's internal affairs. Not even to stop murder, do you believe it?"

"I'm afraid there's more to it than that."

"Enlighten me."

"It's complicated, Ben. Let's wait till we get a table."

It was a sidewalk café. They were shown to a table at a railing protecting the patrons from the pedestrian traffic. Mark ordered chili con queso for them, which he described as one of the world's noblest soups, and tacos de pollo, tortillas rolled into tubes around a filling of shredded chicken, fried until crisp, served with guacamole, a spoonful of heavy sour cream, fried beans, radishes, and onions.

"What do you know about Mexican politics, Ben?"

"Nothing. That scrapbook you saw me carrying is practically my introduction." He told him about the scrapbook.

"General Porfirio Diaz aspires to the presidency," said Mark. "*Aspires* is too weak a word. He'd give his eyeteeth to take over. There'll be a national election next year, but he can't wait. And he's not about to trust his fate to the voters."

"So he's all for assassinating President Lerdo, it's not just Bridget O'Rourke's idea."

"That name rings a bell. Unless I'm mistaken, she's Diaz's mistress."

"You're kidding."

"I'm not. But... getting back to Henry and his unwillingness to help. To begin with he's no great supporter of Lerdo; on the other hand, he's very enthusiastic over Diaz. And very outspoken about it. All he's actually doing is mirroring the trend, the growing American hostility against Lerdo. Lerdo does have his good points: He practices the liberalism he preaches, tries to, but he's the sort of patriot who suspects all foreigners. He has a morbid fear of American capitalists. There are Americans poised at the border willing to put millions of pesos at the disposal of anyone who'd overthrow the government if they get what they want out of it."

"What's that?"

"Everything, Under the pretext of modernizing Mexico, bringing in business and industry, quadrupling railroad mileage. They want to exploit her: silver, iron, every resource she has. It's called progress. They see Diaz as the promise of change, the man who'll sweep Mexico on wings of steam into prosperity. By June of this year the Michoacan war became ruinous; insurrectional movements are festering on all sides; Lerdo is floundering badly."

"So why doesn't Diaz wait for the election?"

"I already told you, he doesn't trust the voters. He's right not to. Besides, he's a man of action. I'm sure he endorses this assassination plot. It was probably his idea."

"It's hers."

"Whosoever. I tell you as a friend: Don't go back to Henry tomorrow expecting that he may have changed his mind. What you told him has gone in one ear and out the other."

"I don't believe it. Lerdo's to be a sacrificial lamb to clear the way to the presidency for Diaz. Suddenly the U.S. is in the business of encouraging assassinations, or at least condoning them."

"Nothing sudden about it. It's been done before, it'll be done again. And don't get down on Henry. He's only acting in what he sees as America's best interests."

"Is that the way you see it?"

"I don't bother to look. It's not my decision."

"You're going to make a first-rate diplomat, Mark."

"Don't get sore. I didn't make the rules, and neither did he. We just play by them."

"I'm going back there with you."

"Didn't he ask you to come back tomorrow morning?"

"I don't care what he asked me, I want that scrapbook back."

"What are you going to do with it?"

"Probably nothing. I just don't want him to have it. He has no right to it."

"You *are* upset, aren't you?"

"Damned right I am."

"I'm sorry, Ben."

"Oh, hell, it's not your fault. What am I taking it out on you for?"

"You do owe me one. You never did get even for my setting that bucket on top of your door, dousing you in your best Sunday suit. Of course, I never would have done it if you hadn't stuck that snake in my bed. I could have died!"

"Blacksnakes are harmless."

"Of fright, idiot." He was looking at Ben fondly, as if he couldn't have wished for a better friend to drop out of the sky and back into his life. "Where are you staying in town?"

"I still have to get a room."

"Don't even bother to look. Every hotel is full up and will be all week. You won't even find a bed in a private home. Independence Day in Mexico is like Mardi Gras week in New Orleans."

As proof, the popping of firecrackers punctuated his words. They were not the first Ben had heard. Bunting and banners were already up on storefronts and buildings, and on the way to the embassy he had seen workmen putting the finishing touches on the bandstand in Zócalo Plaza.

"You can bunk with me," said Mark.

"I'd hate to intrude."

"You'd be company, my honored guest, if you don't mind sleeping on the couch. It's comfortable. My room's on the fourth floor. You can come and go the back way so you won't run into Henry. I'll okay it with the guard. That's settled. Now, what about your dad?"

"I don't know where he is, but he can take care of himself. He'll rough it as usual. He could sleep in a horse trough. I'm sure he has."

"What are you going to do about the assassination?"

"I don't know, Mark. I was counting on the ambassador. I did figure he'd see it as a sticky situation, but I thought he'd at least try to do something. I must be naive. I really thought helping to stop an assassination would be in the best interests of the United States. I'll think of something when I catch up with Cutler. He's disguised as a priest."

"You're in luck. There'll only be about six thousand in town."

"Not one-eyed ones. That's my only edge. He can wear dark glasses or a patch, but either is a dead giveaway. There's really no way he can hide it. Still, maybe Bridget O'Rourke's the one I should look for. I've got her picture in my bag." He smiled thinly. "Should I confide in you? Can I trust you?"

"What do you think? I can help. Besides, we go back a long way. If you need encouragement to make up your mind, you'll be glad to hear that Henry isn't overly fond of me. People are always praising dad to him, and the great job he did. He was offered the ambassadorship before Henry, when U.S. presence here was upgraded from consulate to embassy, but turned it down in favor of retiring. I can see in Henry's eye that he resents Otterbourg Junior. Where do we start?"

"Let's put Cutler and Bridget aside for the moment and concentrate on my father. If he gets to Cutler first, he'll shoot to kill. In front of a thousand witnesses if need be."

"Very determined fellow. He could get into a lot of trouble. The Mexicans get very upset with Americans who take the law into their own hands."

"He knows, he doesn't care. I sometimes think he'd willingly sacrifice his own life to get Cutler."

"Well, whatever you decide, count me in."

"No, Mark. No thanks. It's too risky. You could lose your job. It sounds like Wilson's just looking for an excuse to get rid of you."

"So they'll transfer me. It's not the end of the world. Make up your mind, Ben, are we co-conspirators or do you sleep in an alley for the next three nights?" He offered his hand.

"You haven't changed a hair, Otterbourg." They shook. "Thank the Lord."

They finished lunch with café con leche. They walked back to the embassy. Mark showed him his room. The couch neither looked nor felt quite as comfortable as he had described it but would be far preferable to an alley or park bench. Listening to Mark's litany of conveniences that were readily available to embassy guests, Ben wondered how Bert was making out. At two-thirty, when Mark went back to work, Ben called on Henry Lane Wilson a second time. He asked for the scrapbook back. The ambassador reacted in surprise, then his face darkened with resentment. But he gave it to him.

Twenty

Bert tried four hotels; all were fully booked. He pleaded, cajoled, threatened, and carried on so, demanding a room at the Hotel Montejo, that the assistant manager summoned two burly bellboys who promptly threw him out onto the sidewalk. He resolved to change tactics. He found the grimiest-looking restaurant in the central area and sat down to a bowl of chili. The floor and windowsill alongside his table were alive with cockroaches. Traffic was heavy and ignored by the other patrons. To the surprise of four of them seated nearby, he deftly captured six of the larger cockroaches, imprisoning them in his handkerchief. He paid his bill and left, going straight to the most luxurious hotel in the area, the Camino Real on Mariano Escobedo.

The lobby was impressively columned, furnished with dignity and enviable good taste. He approached the desk, his six captives tucked securely in his outside breast pocket to prevent them from being accidentally crushed.

"ReservationforMr.LloydTevisSanFrancisco."

The desk clerk's eyes reflected alarm.

"Pardóneme?"

"ReservationMr.LloydTevisSanFrancisco."

"Loytevisan Francisco?"

The clerk picked up a clipboard. Upside down Bert read the heading "Reservations." Under it was a long list of names.

"Lemme see that." He snatched it from him. The clerk protested; Bert pulled it away as the man reached to retrieve it. "Here it is, plain as the nose on your face. Edgar Crombie..."

"Crombie? You did not say Crombie, señor...."

"I did so. What are you, deaf? Gimme the register there; lemme sign in for cripes' sakes. Haven't got all day."

He had laid the clipboard with the list on the counter. The clerk snatched it up.

"You said Loytevis..."

"I said Edgar Crombie, plain as day!"

An elderly man with a fierce-looking mustache came bustling up. "What's the trouble, Sanchez?"

"The trouble is, I'm tryin' to register, and this pipsqueak won't let me. My name's right there on that list in his hand: Edgar Crombie, Dallas, Texas. I keep tellin' him—"

"He did not say—" blurted the clerk.

"Never mind. The gentleman obviously has a reservation. Let him sign the register and be done with it." he proferred the pen. Bert scrawled a totally illegible signature with a flourish. "We hope you will enjoy your stay at the Hotel Camino Real, Señor Crombie. We thank you for honoring us with your presence."

He struck the bell summoning the bellboy hard enough to stab his palm and glared at the clerk. The man was standing to one side, glowering at Bert.

• • • •

Two minutes after Bert closed the door on the heels of the bellboy, he strode to the bed and pulled back the coverlet.

Death In Durango

He got out his handkerchief containing his six captives, loosened the knot, and, lifting the pillow, dropped them onto the bed. Then set the pillow on top of them. He then ran to the door and down the stairs to the lobby. The clerk scowled at the sight of him. Bert ignored him and called to the manager.

"Hey, you! What kinda hotel you call this? What are ya runnin' here?"

"Señor, señor, please kindly lower your voice. This is the Camino Real—"

"I know what it is. And you know what you got? *Cucarachas.* Cockroaches! That's what!" Bert boomed.

The man's eyes bulged as he paled visibly. *"Impossible!"*

"See for yourself!"

"Please, I beseech you, lower your voice."

People standing around the lobby were staring at them.

"Come upstairs," said Bert.

Two of the cockroaches had fled, but the other four still occupied the bed. The manager took one look and very nearly suffered a stroke. His hand went to his heart and he staggered backward. He waved his free hand, trying to erase the hideous sight.

"Madre de Dios!"

"You 'spect me to stay in a room fulla cockroaches at these prices? This is a outrage! Ya oughta be 'shamed o' yourselves, chargin' folks to sleep in beds fulla cockroaches with diseases and poisons and God knows what. Disgustin'! I'm not stayin' here one more minute—"

"Mr. Crombie, please keep your voice down. You are disturbing the other guests."

"Don't ya think they got a right to know? And what about these vermin disturbin' me? Gimme 'nother room, and pronto!"

"My dear sir, there are no other rooms. The hotel is fully booked."

"Then gimme your room!"

"My dear sir, that is impossible. Where are you going?"

"Down to the lobby. And spread the word; tell folks what kinda place you're runnin' here, the Hotel Cockroach!"

"My dear sir, I implore you, do not reveal this. Upon my word of honor, the housekeeping is immaculate, our staff the finest in the city. But accidents do happen...."

He finally succeeded in calming him down and exacting his promise not to breathe a word to other guests. The prize for his silence was a small room with a brand-new bed, top-floor rear. To Bert it proved that the best-laid plans of mice and men are not always doomed to failure. His plan, concocted as he sat downing his chili in the restaurant, was based on the knowledge that all hotels, regardless of how heavy the demand for reservations, always keep one or two rooms vacant and available in a genuine emergency. Eventually, possibly within the hour, the real Edgar Crombie of Dallas, Texas, would show up. His arrival would greatly confuse the clerk and the manager, until it dawned on them that they had been duped. But the cockroaches were real and a calamitous threat to the hotel's reputation, and the commotion Bert was certain to raise if they were to attempt to evict him threatened to be just as calamitous.

He sat on his bed mulling over strategy for tracking down Cutler. Mexico City boasted a population of close to three hundred thousand during normal times. The holiday could add at least half again as many visitors. Including priests. If only there was some way to bring them together in a body. The climax of the celebration on the sixteenth would, but what could he do to accomplish it before then?

He thought and thought about it but could not come up with anything resembling a practical idea. Around four in the afternoon he was preparing to leave to go looking for the needle in the haystack, was actually at the door with one foot over the sill when he looked down.

Just in time to see a cockroach scurrying down the hall.

• • • •

Ben set about his search with Bridget O'Rourke's photograph removed from its frame and tucked in his pocket, showing it to everyone he approached, at the same time keeping an eye out for Bert and Cutler. By late afternoon of the next day, Tuesday, he decided that the haystack was much too large to poke through. If any luck were to come his way, it would do so on Thursday the sixteenth. Mark Otterbourg agreed.

"Even if you find her, what can you do? Getting her arrested won't help you find Cutler."

"How do I get her arrested? On what charge, suspicion? If I go around spouting off about assassination, I'll be the one they'll lock up. On suspicion of insanity."

They sat in Mark's room talking. The single window overlooked the rose garden at the rear of the embassy. Ambassador Wilson was out in apron and gloves, his sleeves rolled up, pruning bushes, looking more like a gentleman gardener than the captain of America's presence in Mexico. Ben got up from the couch and looked down at him. He was the key, he thought, but refused to be inserted and turned. He could get to President Lerdo and warn him, show him the scrapbook, suggest precautions that could be taken. Mark had told him that Lerdo had a double who sometimes filled in for him on state occasions, an actor who carried himself identically, displayed the same obese torso, small jaw, and skinny legs, and who had purposely had his head shaved to duplicate the president's baldness. Hearing of this, Ben's eyes widened.

"Substituting his double would be perfect!"

"Not for the double. And if he did take his place and was shot and killed, everybody would think Lerdo knew about the plot beforehand and deliberately sent the fellow to his death to protect himself. Not exactly the ideal image the people should have of their president."

"I guess. Any ideas?"

"Maybe. Tell me, does Cutler speak Spanish?"

"To tell the truth I don't know. He could and fluently; he's bright enough."

"Then right now he could be mingling with other priests, posing as a visitor, attaching himself to the cathedral staff or one of the churches. You said that he's posed as a cleric before; he probably knows the ropes and can impersonate one without raising anyone's suspicions. If all that's so, why don't we make the rounds of the churches?"

"How many are there?"

"About sixty."

"Oh, Lord. It'd take us a month. Another thing: The street names change every block. It's the most confusing city I've ever seen."

"See how badly you need me? We can check out the bigger churches: La Profesa, Loreto, Santa Teresa, Santa Domingo, San Hipolito..."

"I don't know, Mark. Why would he bother? Everywhere you look, you see priests and nuns wandering about sightseeing. It's so easy for him to lose himself in the crowd, even with dark glasses or an eye patch. And there's no reason for the two of them to stick together."

"There's a huge parade Independence Day afternoon. Church people march in and stand under the palace balcony when the president speaks."

"Cutler'll be there..."

"You've never seen so many priests and nuns in a single group before. Thousands."

"It still has to be better than wandering around the city looking for him. I wonder where he's staying? With somebody? Are others involved in the plot? Or will he be working alone? He usually does. He doesn't need help in something like this."

"Standing below the balcony when he fires, he'll give himself away on the spot. He'll be about forty feet away from Lerdo. He'll get off two, maybe only one, shot before he's grabbed."

"He's very good, Mark. One shot'll be all he'll need."

"He must know he'll never get away—"

"You underestimate him. If he can disguise his gun, shoot at the ideal moment, when everybody's cheering, everybody's arms are raised, he can fire, drop the gun, kick it away. He's very capable, extremely clever, and he's got guts."

"Are you going to give up looking until Thursday?"

"I can't. He's probably keeping out of sight, but there's no reason for her to. Knowing her taste, she's got to be staying at one of the best hotels."

"The Stella Maris, the St. Teresa, and the Camino Royal are the most expensive. There isn't a finer hotel in New York City than the Camino Royal."

"If we do fine her, maybe I can break her down, scare her into betraying where he's hiding. Do you have any connections with the local police?"

"You want somebody to back you up in scaring her? I don't know, Ben. Without absolute proof that there's going to be an assassination attempt it'd be risky for them."

"It would."

Ben turned his eyes from the ambassador working in the garden to the scrapbook on a small table. It lay open to Lerdo's crossed-out photo. Should he show the book to the chief of police and tell his story? He sighed. Why bother? He could be allied with Diaz.

• • • •

Confronted with the same problems, Bert was faring no better. By Tuesday evening he, too, resolved that if Cutler was to be caught, it would have to be in the act. It would be dangerous to President Lerdo, but he could see no other options. No sense in trying to talk his way by the guards and get in to see Lerdo. He thought about the American ambassador and decided that Ben had already covered that angle and come up against a blank wall. Ambassadors were, after all, nothing more than appointed politicians, two breeds from the same governmental womb, both full of hot air and promise and woefully short on delivery and spleen.

Every time he walked by the front desk, the clerk and manager glared at him. The fourth time, early Tuesday evening, he was coming back from searching for Cutler, passing the desk, when the manager cleared his throat and signaled that he wanted a word with him. Bert approached the desk. The man was furious, his mustache twitching, eyes blazing. From the look of him Bert half expected his hair to begin rising on end.

His words came at him like bullets. "It may interest you to know that Mr. Edgar Crombie checked in half an hour ago."

"Who?"

"Edgar Crombie, Edgar Crombie."

"Who?"

"Who! Who! You told us *your* name was Edgar Crombie."

"I did not."

"You did. You registered as Edgar Crombie. Look here." The manager flipped the pages of the registration book, found the signature, and spun the book around. "Right there!"

"That's not Edgar Crombie, that's my name, Loytevisharee," he deliberately mumbled.

"What?"

Bert repeated the unintelligible string of syllables.

"I don't understand you. And who can read this signature? It's like a child's scrawl. It could be anything."

"It's my name, Loytevisharee."

"Whatever you call yourself, you did not have a reservation!"

"Then how come ya gimme a room?"

"Because you said your name was Edgar Crombie!"

"Who?"

"Edgar Crombie! Edgar Crombie! Sssssh, keep your voice down, please," the manager pleaded.

"You're the one's mouthin' off. So what are ya goin' to do, throw me out in the street? After all ya put me through with your cockroaches?"

"They were not *our* cockroaches!"

"They weren't mine."

"That was a fluke, a mishap. It could not happen again in a million years."

"Happened to me," Bert said. "Okay, I'll check out. I don't much like the idea o' layin' awake at night wonderin' if a bunch o' your cockroaches are gonna climb in bed to keep me company, anyhow. I don't 'magine your other guests'd like it any better'n me. 'Course, they don't know what happened. By rights they should; they should know so's they can decide whether they wanta put up with six-legged, nonpayin' freeloaders sharin' their walls or not. Somebody oughta wise 'em up. I know you and the rest o' your boys are busy, so maybe I should do it. Camp out on the sidewalk and tell everybody who comes in what happened to me, which you can back me up on. Folks gotta right to know they're registerin' at the Hotel Cockroach, wouldn't ya say? That's what this place is. The best hotel in Mexico City, maybe in the whole entire country, is really the Hotel Cockroach!"

"Stop using that word!" hissed the manager. "And keep your voice down." His eyes narrowed, flashing left and right. "You . . . do not have to leave."

"But I wanna—"

"No, no, no! You will stay. When . . . when did you plan on checking out, Friday?"

"Friday. Be outta here like a shot, but hey, I can leave now."

"No, no, no, no, no!"

"You sure?"

"Yes, please, please, please."

He flung out the backs of his hands like a pair of wounded doves flapping their last. Bert thanked him and started up the stairs. So Edgar Crombie of Dallas, Texas, had arrived, had he? Would he run into a cockroach welcoming committee? Cockroaches sure had a knack for making more cockroaches faster than you can drop your hat.

He stood at the window looking down upon Mariano Escobedo, the heavy traffic, and the building fronts festooned with red, white, and green banners and bunting, and wondered what Ben was up to. He wondered if he was having any better luck.

Thursday dawned bright and clear, a perfect day for the climax of the celebration. The holiday got under way in earnest at eight in the morning. Bands paraded about the city, fireworks were set off in every block, crowds surged about the plaza expectantly, hours before the afternoon's festivities, and the usual army of drunks and near drunks staggered about the central city. At one o'clock a parade that was to stretch nearly a mile began to form in Chapultepec Park, near the castle. It would march down Paseo de la Reforma to El Caballito monument, turn into Avenue Juarez, cross San Juan de Letrán into Avenue Medero to the plaza in front of the National Palace and the balcony where President Lerdo would appear to address the multitudes.

Among the marchers were thousands of priests and nuns. Ben, with Mark Otterbourg, and Bert separately searched the crowd of black-robed clergy in vain.

Bert followed the clergy segment of the parade as best he could from one side of the street; Ben and Mark did so from the other. So congested was it, father and son failed to see each other. Both studied the faces of the priests formed into ranks, each one carrying a cross. Both saw only one priest wearing an eye patch, but he was a foot shorter than Cutler, portly, and at least twenty years older.

Panic began to take root in Bert's heart when the procession turned into La Plaza de la Constitución, the great central square more familiarly known as Zócalo. It had been the political and religious center of Mexico for more than five hundred years. President Lerdo's offices were on the same grounds from which Montezuma had ruled his tribes and the Spanish viceroys directed the affairs of Spain in the New World. The Cathedral stood within the area once encompassed by the great Aztec court. La Catedral de la Asunción de Maria had been built to replace an earlier church and stood in part on the ground once occupied by the *tzompantli,* the Aztec ceremonial skull rack. Construction of the cathedral was ordered by Philip II in 1552, but the actual work was not begun until twenty-one years later. Almost two hundred and fifty years passed before the building was completed. It was the largest church in Mexico, measuring two hundred feet from ground level to the tops of the twin bell towers. Within it were sixteen chapels and twenty-seven altars. A stairway near the west door led to an underground crypt containing more than three thousand burial places, including that of the first archbishop of Mexico.

The Palacio Nacional filled the entire east side of the Zócalo, standing at right angles to the Cathedral. It was originally built by Cortez and subsequently rebuilt in the mid-1500s as a residence for the viceroys of New Spain. Over the central doorway hung the Independence Bell.

When the clergy arrived en masse in the square, the priests and nuns affiliated with the cathedral and local churches assembled separately on the cathedral steps. Visiting priests and nuns mingled with the crowd, the majority of them standing in the forefront with an unobstructed view of the second-floor balcony. Meanwhile Ben and Mark had made their way to the northeast corner, which afforded them a clear view of the front of the crowd.

"There must be at least a couple thousand watching from the cathedral steps," said Mark. "It cuts them down by more than a third."

"It doesn't seem to make any difference," said Ben glumly. "There's no sign of him."

"You *will* recognize him if you spot him."

"In a second."

"You think it's possible there's been a change in plans?"

"Not a chance. He's coming. What am I saying?—he's here. I just don't see him. I wonder where Bert is."

Bert wondered where Ben was. He had shouldered his way through the crowd and was standing in the forefront, surrounded by nuns and priests. President Lerdo had not yet appeared. A rope descended from the center of the balcony railing to the bell below, awaiting his hand. The first ring of it is going to be your death knell, mused Bert grimly, if the hole card doesn't turn up pretty quick.

His eyes traveled from one priest's face to another. Every one looked as innocent as a baby, with not a fleeting thought of assassination lurking behind their eyes. Six different bands had invaded the area, blaring loud cacophony, each trying to be heard over the others. A cannon was fired three times, sharply cutting off the music and stilling the crowd.

Bert continued to search faces. Was Cutler still wearing his Durango beard? he wondered. Was he still even dressed as a priest? What was he covering his absent eye with? A patch? Dark glasses? A bandage? His heart thudded wildly and nearly burst from his chest as a group appeared overhead on the balcony. One of them, whom he assumed to be President Lerdo, stepped to the railing and waved his arms. He was not at all impressing-looking: bald, clean-shaven, with watery eyes and a belly much too large for his otherwise underdeveloped frame. He wore a red, green, and white sash under his dark blue jacket, a matching bow tie, and high, starched collar. Were it not for the sash, he could easily be taken for a bank teller.

Still Bert examined faces, shouldering his way rudely about, eliciting glares and frowns. Where was Diaz, he wondered, six miles from town on his way in at the head of six thousand men armed to the teeth? Probably. Where was Bridget O'Rourke? Standing somewhere in the rear of the crowd with a flag under her arm, ready to raise it in triumph the instant Lerdo went down with a bullet through the heart?

He watched him and pitied him. He may not have been impressive-looking, but there was no trace of cruelty or lust for power in his expression. Bert had no idea what sort of president he was, how capable, how honest, how caring about his people, but he certainly presented the appearance of a sensitive human being.

With about twenty seconds to live!

He had lowered his arms, dissolved his smile, and cleared his throat, preparing to speak. He started. At the end of his second sentence, not a word of which Bert understood, the crowd roared approvingly; even the nuns and priests raised their arms and voiced their good feelings toward him. Bert continued to concentrate on faces. He moved to his left, excusing himself in English, pushing his face into one face after another. Those he challenged instinctively drew back in surprise.

President Lerdo rattled on enthusiastically. The crowd raised a second cheer of approval. Up came everyone's arms. Bert's eyes fixed on a tall nun. She stood head and shoulders above the other nuns around her. He could not see her face, positioned as he was to her right and slightly behind her. It was her right arm that caught his attention. It was stiff, strange-looking, and seemed to be paralyzed. Her hand looked to be carved of stone.

He lunged and grabbed her. A shot rang; both hands gripped her forearm and pulled it toward him. The bullet went straight up into the air. Women screamed, men bellowed; panic struck on all sides.

And her arm came off in his hands.

Twenty-one

Pandemonium reigned, the square exploding with excitement. Momentarily stunned by the object in his hand—a forearm and hand fashioned of plaster, the arm hollow and containing a Smith & Wesson American .44, the muzzle passing through the wrist to the palm of the hand, a small hole in the center of it—Bert stood transfixed. Cutler fled, slipping through the crowd. Bert came to life just in time to catch sight of him looking back with one baleful eye. He was wearing wire-rimmed spectacles, his right eye socket concealed behind a clouded lens, the left lens perfectly clear.

Bert took off after him but needn't have bothered. Cutler did not get fifteen feet from him before the nuns and priests closed in tightly around him, blocking his escape. Policemen, wearing formal powder-blue uniforms and white gloves for the celebration, came rushing up, guns drawn. They quickly took him prisoner. Bert followed as they marched him away; others, the curious, also followed until the sergeant in charge turned and barked them to a halt. Still holding the fake arm containing the gun, Bert stood watching Cutler depart with his captors. The sergeant suddenly stopped them, turned, came back, and took the arm from him.

"*Evidencia!*"

"Yeah, and evidence too. Lock him up and throw 'way the key. . . . Cripes' sakes!"

He jerked off his hat and slammed it to the ground. Ben and Mark came running up.

"Bert!"

"Some fine kettle o' fish this is! Now I can't no more get at him than I can the King o' Siam. If this doesn't beat all!"

"You captured him!" burst Ben.

"You saved the president's life!" burst Mark.

"You're a hero!" cried Ben.

In testimony of which people began crowding around Bert, clapping him on the back, seizing and pumping his hands. He ignored them.

"I coulda plugged him in the act if I coulda found him. What stinkin' luck! They wind up hangin' him, and I wind up holdin' the sack as usual. Damn! Who's he?" he asked, scowling at Ben.

Ben introduced Mark. At mention of Ambassador Henry Lane Wilson, Bert stiffened defensively.

"Ya talked to him and come up empties; I tolja ya would; didn't I tell ya you'd be wastin' your time? Come on, let's follow that bunch and see where they're takin' him. . . ."

"To the Ascención Street jail, most likely," said Mark. "It's the closest."

Ben looked about them. "Keep your eyes peeled for Bridget, Bert. She could show up there the same time he does."

"Don't mean beans to me; they can shoot themselves silly for all I care. Cutler's the only one I'm innerested in. I had him and lost him."

"Wonderful! Marvelous!" Ben threw up his hands.

"What's bitin' you?"

"You're no different than Wilson. Neither of you has the

slightest interest in the attempted assassination. Do me a favor and don't knock him to me; in your own way you're as bad as he is."

"Oh, yeah? Maybe it's high time you started thinkin' 'bout what's number one on the list, what we're down here for."

"Just because this attempt failed is no reason to think she won't try again," said Mark.

"You bet she will," said Ben. "Let's get over to the station and tell whoever's in charge what's going on. I can give them her picture; they'll pick her up."

"Will you sign a complaint against her?" Mark asked.

"In a minute."

"Aw for cripes' sakes, who cares 'bout her? What we gotta do should be as clear as the nose on your face: get over there and get him sprung. How, I dunno, but we should be able to come up with somethin' by the time we get there. I sure can't plug him through his cell window, that's for sure. Too risky."

Mark was staring at Ben with frightened eyes. Ben dismissed his concern with a wave.

"Don't pay any attention to him, he's just blowing off steam as usual. Come on."

• • • •

The three of them, along with dozens of others, were refused admittance to the station, a bull-chested sergeant ordering them to go about their business. Bert's protest ended abruptly when the sergeant pulled his gun. They started up the street toward the American Embassy. A two-seated surrey drew up alongside them, and two bearded gentlemen in formal attire, complete with top hats, beckoned Bert over. The upshot of the ensuing conversation was that President Lerdo wanted Bert to come to the palace so that he could thank him in person for saving his life. Bert puffed his chest like an Atwater prairie chicken going into its mating dance, leered in triumph at Ben, and magnanimously invited him and Mark to come along.

Death In Durango

• • • •

President Sebastian Lerdo de Tejada, looking unruffled in spite of his brush with death less than a half hour before, sat in an intricately carved crested chair with padded seat rails and legs with casters by an open window, watching the swarming crowds below in the plaza, waiting, it appeared, for the sun to set and the fireworks display to begin. Ben's second impression was that he was deliberately offering his opposition another shot at him. He rose from his chair as they came into the room with their two escorts. The president did not speak English, but one of the men who had brought them, a Colonel Ignacia Mejía, Minister of War, volunteered to act as interpreter. Lerdo's professions of gratitude were brief but came from the heart. He then revealed that telegrams would soon be dispatched: President Grant would be the first American north of the border to know of Señor Slaughter's heroism. Other high officials in Washington would also be apprised. A messenger was at that very moment carrying a handwritten note to Ambassador Henry Lane Wilson apprising him of the incident. Señor Slaughter's gallant role would be heralded in every newspaper on the continent.

"Tell him thanks, and ask him if he could do us a small favor," said Bert to the colonel.

"Name it."

"How's 'bout releasin' the 'sassin into our custody so's we can bring him back to Frisco to stand trial for prev'ous murders and robb'ries and such which is what we come down here to do in the first place, corral him and fetch him back."

As he listened, the furrows in the colonel's ivory brow hinted that he did not completely understand everything Bert was saying, but what he did he promptly translated for the president. Lerdo sat tenting his fingers, pondering his answer. When he responded, the colonel nodded agreement.

"His Excellency would prefer that the accused be kept incarcerated here. To permit him to leave the country in your custody might not sit well with the people. An attempt to assassinate His Excellency is a criminal affront to the state, and the people *are* the state. You understand..."

"Yeah, sure, only—"

"Bert," interrupted Ben, "let them keep him. He'll be tried, found guilty, and hanged."

"That's good 'nough for you, maybe, but it stinks with me!"

"Bert—"

"Don't 'Bert' me. What ails you, anyhow? You know, if you'd'a been with me, 'steada off skylarkin', together we mighta hung onto him. If I'd'a grabbed his other arm, he wouldn't'a got away...."

"If you had, he'd have gotten off an accurate shot. We'll talk about it later!"

Ben's clenched teeth and his icy tone startled Bert, quieting him. Ben got out Bridget O'Rourke's picture, unfolding it and handing it to Colonel Mejía. He inserted a monocle in his right eye and studied it. And nodded.

"Señora O'Rourke, Diaz's paramour."

"She organized the attempt. Hired Cutler and brought him down here from Durango. She may still be here."

"I'll alert the security police to pick her up, although she's probably already on her way out of the country."

President Lerdo was intrigued by the plaster arm and hand containing the gun that Cutler had used to conceal the attempt. Bert and Ben both credited him with cleverness and ingenuity, but Ben was convinced that the device was Bridget's idea, as was changing Cutler's disguise from a priest to a nun.

"They both knew we'd follow them down and be looking for a priest. The woman's as brilliant as she is ruthless."

"She is devoted to Diaz," said the colonel. "She would die for him. When we catch her, we'll be pleased to offer her the opportunity."

The president pulled a velvet cord summoning a servant. In he came, treading soundlessly, carrying a velvet pillow on which a small rectangular box reposed. His Excellency took it from him, opened it, and displayed the contents: a gold medal with the red, green, and white colors of Mexico on the attached ribbon. It bore the likeness of Miguel Hidalgo y Costilla, father of Mexican independence. It was dated September 27, 1821, Independence Day.

"My country's most valued and prestigious decoration. I hereby aware the Medal of Independence to you, Señor Slaughter, for your courageous act."

Bert blushed slightly as he pinned it to his pocket.

"Thank ya, Mr. Pres'dent, it was nothin', but I was glad to do it."

"Now, if you will do us the honor of stepping out onto the balcony and sounding the Independence bell. In the more than fifty years of our freedom as a sovereign nation, you will be the first non-Mexican to do so."

The president, Colonel Mejía, and the other dignitary applauded. Bert hesitated. He seemed to stiffen. Ben got the impression that he was reluctant to step out onto the balcony for fear of being shot at.

"Bert..."

"Yeah, yeah."

They adjourned to the balcony. President Lerdo summoned the crowd's attention, introduced Bert to tumultuous applause and cheering, ceremoniously handed him the bell rope, and stood aside.

And Bert Slaughter, American citizen, his newly acquired decoration for heroism gleaming on his chest, rang the bell celebrating Mexican independence, wondering as he did so what Lloyd Tevis would think when he heard the news.

Twenty-two

"Extraordinary, absolutely extraordinary. To think that you were able to spot him in such a disguise among so many of them dressed indentically is amazing. My dear chap, this single act will do more for relations between our two countries then the lifting of embargoes, dollar diplomacy, the most generous concessions on both sides, glad hands across the border.... My dear chap, you're the man of the hour. Had we suspected than an attempt to assassinate His Excellency was afoot, rest assured we would have assisted in every possible way."

Ben winced, unable to believe his hearing. He decided on the spot that Ambassador Wilson's gall recognized no limitations. How he could make such an outrageous statement in his presence astounded Ben. He could not resist exchanging glances with Mark Otterbourg. Mark smiled thinly. The three of them had come from the palace to the embassy accompanied by Colonel Mejía and preceded by President Lerdo's hand-delivered note to the ambassador.

Ben fought down the urge to puncture Wilson's balloon, release the hot air in a loud *whoosh*, deflate him completely before the colonel and Mark. But why bother? Why antagonize him, and why cast a shadow over Bert's hour of glory?

"I intend to contact your superiors at Wells Fargo in San Francisco," Wilson went on. "The entire world will know of your heroism. May I ask, Albert—"

"Just Bert."

"Of course. Where are you staying?"

"Hotel Camino Real." Up went Ben's eyebrows. Mark gasped.

"How the devil did you get in there?" asked Ben.

"Easy. Made friends with the lady at the desk, charmed the heels clean off her shoes. Ya know me, son—when I turn on the ol' personal'ty, women can't resist me. Oh, she didn't gimme the bridal suit or anything, it's just a little room top-floor rear, but comfor'ble, comfor'ble. Where'd you light?"

Ben eyed the ambassador. "I found a place not far from here," he lied.

"Would you both do us the honor of being our guests here at the embassy for the duration of your stay?" Wilson asked.

"That's mighty gen'rous o' ya," said Bert, "but we'll be pullin' out tomorrow. Ya could do us a favor, though." He glanced at the colonel, then back to the ambassador. "This would-be 'sassin Cutler, we'd really and truly like to take him back with us. He's 'merican, ya know."

He went on to explain in detail. Ben watched the colonel; Bert's request did not appear to nettle him. A knock sounded, interrupting him. It was an officer in the black-and-red uniform of the security police. He apologized for interrupting, whispered briefly to Colonel Mejía, and went back out. Bad news, decided Ben, studying the colonel's rapidly darkening expression. Bert resumed talking.

"Wells Fargo's been after Cutler for fifteen years—"

"Excuse me, Mr. Slaughter," said the colonel, "I'm afraid I have distressing news."

"He's escaped," said Ben.

"Yes."

Bert started and stared in shocked disbelief. "No!"

The colonel nodded. "It appears Mrs. O'Rourke lost no time in arranging things. Two men in security-police uniforms appeared at the station house in Ascención Street, showed the captain in charge an order with the forged signature of the chief of security, Cutler was released in their custody, purportedly to be transferred to the state prison, and all three have disappeared into thin air."

"I knew it! I knew it, I knew it, I knew it!" Bert smashed his hat to the floor and snatched it up. "Let's go, son, let's get outta here. Outta this dumb city, this friggin' fourth-rate, secon'-class country!" He glared at the colonel. "Got him under lock and key, police all 'round him, and let him walk out free as a bird. If this don't beat all! If this isn't the straw what busted the camel's back, I dunno what is!"

"Bert, calm down—"

"Shut up! Ya comin' or not? Don't! Stay here and twiddle your thumbs and sit lookin' like a ninny for all I care. I'm gone!"

Out he stomped, slamming the door behind him so hard that the Stars and Stripes tacked to the wall over the oriel window came loose, the upper right-hand tack falling out. Ben threw up his hands. Ambassador Wilson stared wide-eyed at the door. Mark stared at his feet and slowly shook his head. Colonel Mejía looked thoroughly confused. Ben rose from his chair.

"I apologize for him. He does have a tendency to explode. If you'll excuse me, I'll go catch up with him. Hopefully I can calm him down, get him to listen to reason. Hopefully," Ben said, with an expression that clearly testified that there was no such hope.

Outside there was no sign of Bert. Ben and Mark did find his medal on the floor. The pin was bent, and a piece of material from Bert's shirt clung to it. Ben picked up the medal and put it in his pocket.

Twenty-three

Ben accompanied Bert back to San Francisco. After Bert had fled the embassy he squandered the rest of the day and the next two in a fruitless search of the city, ignoring and duplicating the efforts of the local police and the state security police. However, he was unable to ignore his grateful and adoring public. Everywhere he searched he was recognized, congratulated, embraced, kissed, and hailed as *la Yanqui hero*! A mariachi band followed him about, drinks were thrust into his hand when he walked by *cantinás*, food was offered him on the street, flowers were flung at him. A ten-foot effigy fashioned of roses and feathers was set upon a pedestal in the plaza on the very spot where he had performed his heroic act. He trailed children like the legendary Pied Piper of Hamelin; churchmen blessed him and pressed crucifixes into his hand; men set upon him like fanatical sports fans, raising him to their shoulders and parading him about; women proposed marriage, and one had herself delivered to his hotel naked and rolled up in a hand-loomed rug as the Queen of the Nile. At the insistence of the owners, the manager of the Camino Real threw open the doors of the hotel's sumptuous bridal suite to him for Friday and Saturday nights—no charge. He was king of the mountain, man of the hour, the fair-haired hero, savior of the republic, Hercules and Galahad. Mexico was his theater, Mexico City the stage, the spotlight focused on Egbert Wallace Arlo Slaughter. Its radiance and the adulation it attracted did not distract him from his purpose, however. He persisted in his search, combing the city, satisfying himself at the end of the two days plus that the bird had flown.

Bridget O'Rourke did not turn up. Their own separate search unavailing, the police decided that the two of them had gotten back together and were heading for Oaxaco, two hundred and fifty miles to the southeast where Profiro Diaz had retired in the late sixties to tend the baneful bramble of his ambition and await the propitious hour when he would rise and usurp the reins of government, but a check with the Oaxaco authorities established that neither Cutler nor Bridget had shown up there as yet.

Ben did not think they'd get back together; there was no need, unless she was planning a second attempt on President Lerdo's life. Even if she were, knowing Cutler as he had come to, he couldn't imagine *he* would try again. Still he, Ben, saw nothing to deter *her;* Mexico was overrun with hireable *norteamericano* guns. Why she'd bothered to go out of the country to engage Cutler in the first place was beyond him. Yes, she would try again. If anything, she was even more fanatical than her late husband.

The train had left San José en route to San Francisco. Bert had just finished putting his foot down for perhaps the thirtieth time. He stoutly refused even to consider returning to the Wells Fargo fold. He maintained that having had a taste of the chase, he much preferred it to the obligations of a steady job. He liked being "his own man" for a change and declared his intention of continuing the arrangement.

He also declared that the loss of Cutler was "Purely temp'rary."

The train sped through the patchwork quilt of neatly tended farms and orchards, drawing closer to the bay. Their car was only half full; the day was magnificent, despite all of Bert's efforts to cloud it over with complaining. Ben had long ago developed the ability to close his ears when his father began complaining. To listen to him was one of the more insidious forms of self-abuse. He never ran out of wind and never stopped repeating himself, boring everyone within range of his voice to tears. No longer did Ben even half listen. He had heard it all so often, he could practically recite it from memory, for whatever the object of Bert's scorn, however disparate one grumble from another, he poured forth the same speech. By San José, however, he began to show signs of wearying of listening to himself. A good sign, thought Ben, a welcome sign. He'd also pinned his medal back on, explaining that it wasn't President Lerdo's fault that Cutler had gotten away.

"Yes, sir, pure temp'rary."

Ben marveled—out of the nearly two thousand miles of complaining sprang the flower of optimism. Of course, without it there would be no sense in even thinking about continuing the pursuit.

"Any hunches on where he's gotten to?" he asked.

"Whattaya think? He's sure not gonna hang 'round down there. What for? He's got himself a bigger ax hangin' over his head than we hung. No, he'll be back in the States if he's not already, which he prob'ly is. Not back to Cal'fornia, though."

"Where?"

"Whattaya think, I got a crystal ball or somethin'? How should I know? All we can do is keep a eye on the newspapers. Sooner or later he'll turn up; always has. And while we're on the subjec' there's a little something I been meanin' to set you straight on. From here on in I'll handle him alone."

"Sure."

"I mean it, Ben. Watchin' you op'rate, hearin' what you

say, it's as plain as the nose on your face that ya got no heart for gunnin' him down like he should be. Like it's written in the stars he's gonna be. If you were to get him in a corner, ya'd capture him, push him in front of a judge and jury. If I letcha, which I don't intend to, because if ya did, I'd likely get so mad I'd put a bullet through ya, which I wouldn't wanna do. No, sir, from now on he's all mine, 'sclusive. Do ya'self and me a favor and stay outta it. Promise?"

"Cross my heart."

"Liar! What did I ever do to deserve a son I raised my own self to be a liar?"

"Will you keep your voice down?"

"I mean it, Ben. I'll go far as Frisco with ya, but when we get there, you and me are quits. Not perm'nant; I'm not sore atcha, nothin' pers'nal, only that I'm goin' after him alone. You, you go back to work for the wolf—"

"In snake's clothing."

"Right."

"Right. Without you."

"By yourself. They'll pair ya up with somebody cap'ble'; ya got ta fairly decent track record; James Hume won't throw ya to the wolves. I'll stay in touch."

"Very considerate of you."

"I don't mind, we're flesh and blood. We shouldn't let too much grass grow between us."

"And after you kill Cutler you'll come back to work."

"Not for Tevis, not in four million years o' Mondays," Bert said. "Never. I've gotta belly fulla his sneaky ways, his double- and triple-crossin'. Insults and sarcasm. Ya know something?"

"What?"

"Him and me don't like each other."

"Really?"

"Really."

"He did send the ransom money down to Durango."

"James Hume and John Valentine twisted his arm, ya betcha."

"He didn't have to. You'd severed relations with the

Death In Durango

company. Yet he sent a letter of credit for ten thousand dollars. A tidy sum."

"When ya see him, tell him thanks."

"Say, I almost forgot, James will be at the station to welcome us. When you got off to get the paper in Bakersfield, I sent him a wire."

"Whaja do that for!"

"I promised him I'd stay in touch. He's your friend, Bert, one of the best, if not *the* best, you've ever had."

"Awww..."

"He's a sensitive and considerate soul; he cares. He came down to see me off. He didn't have to. He'll be there to welcome us; be nice to him. Try to smile for a change."

"Got nothin' to smile about. I can smile with the best of 'em when there's something to smile for, but I don't see anything to smile for in this mess o' slops: His flyin' the coop, her gettin' off scot-free, me nearly gettin' my ticket punched by Suarez and the cops in Nombre de Dios, white scorpions and kidnappin', rotten food, iron bars, saddles sores, sunstroke, and the Hotel Cockroach."

"The what?"

"Nothin'."

Bert lay back in the corner of his seat and tilted his hat down over his face. Just before he started snoring, his left hand reached up to his breast pocket to cover his medal covetously.

• • • •

John Valentine sat across from James B. Hume in the latter's office. Hume was holding Ben's telegram, dispatched earlier in the day from Bakersfield.

"Their train is due in at 2:05," he said. "I'm going over to Union Station to meet them. Want to come along?"

"Wouldn't miss it for the world. Egbert'll be so puffed up, he won't be able to squeeze his chest through the door.

Wonder if his feet have touched ground yet," Valentine mused.

"He's got every right to be proud; evidently he was in the right place at the right time. Congratulatory telegrams came pouring in from all over. Mr. Tevis even got one from Governor-General Dufferin of Canada this morning."

"A week late. I'm fond of Egbert, admire him, but you have to admit that he is the unlikeliest hero in modern history. This whole foofaraw strikes me as like dressing Lucretia Borgia up as Joan of Arc and setting her on a white horse."

"Hardly," Hume said.

"Never a dull moment with Egbert."

The door opened. It was Albertina Preble, Hume's secretary. "Excuse me, sir, four more welcome-home telegrams. Another from the president, from Vice-President Wilson, Governor Irwin, and the Mexican Ambassador in Washington. This has been the most exciting week! They say he's coming in today. The whole building's in an uproar; it's worse than when we first got word!"

Lloyd Tevis brushed by her without excusing himself and came in. "What the devil is going on around this place? Everybody jabbering, carrying on like old home week, nobody working that I can see...."

Hume waved Ben's wire. "They're due in at 2:05. John and I are going over to the station. Want to come?"

"I don't think so," said Tevis testily. "He certainly doesn't expect me on the welcoming committee. Oh, I know what he did, and more power to him, I guess; but I see no reason for everybody to go loony all over again. It's been a week—"

"Four more telegrams came in," interposed Miss Preble.

"I know, I know. The fact remains that he's no longer employed by this company. Why are we all getting so stirred up?"

"I'm not," said Hume mildly. "Are you, John?"

"Not a bit."

"Not much," snapped Tevis. "I seem to be the only one keeping things in perspective."

"It is rather exciting," said Valentine.

"Go welcome him home if you want, only don't bring him back here. He and I have nothing to say to each other; his association with this company is history. He owes us nothing, and we don't owe him a red cent."

"Was there something you wanted to see me about, sir?" Hume asked.

"I—drat! Damned if I can remember! This really is the limit; a man can't even think straight around this madhouse."

Out he stormed. Hume consulted his watch as John Valentine took the telegrams from Miss Preble.

"Ten minutes to one. Shall we have lunch then stroll over to the station?"

"Let's."

● ● ● ●

They were ten minutes out of San Francisco when Bert awoke from his nap.

Ben eyed him questioningly.

"There's something I've been meaning to ask you. How *did* you manage to get a hotel room, and in the Camino Royale of all places? You certainly didn't charm the desk clerk out of one. How did you wangle it?"

"Ya want the honest truth?"

"Assuming it's possible."

"Don't be sarcastic. The truth is that it was bald luck. I was goin' up to the desk, right behind a fella and his missus, couple o' out-o'-towners, and they were cancelin' their reservation. Something about a death in the fam'ly back in Dallas. I was Johnny-on-the-spot. I stepped up after 'em and asked for the reservation. The clerk didn't wanna give it to me, natur'ly, I mean, right outta the blue. I hadda slip him twenny bucks."

"Twenty dollars? You? I don't believe it."

"You sayin' I'm tight-fisted?"

"You're so tight, silver melts in your hand."

"You're forgettin', it wasn' my money." Ben glared. "That place wasn't the lap o' lux'ry everybody makes it out to be, either. Oh, it's highfalutin, and spit and polish, and 'spensive, and there was no ring 'round the wash sink, but there's cockroaches...."

"In the Camino Royale? I don't believe that, either."

"There is."

Now, reflected Bert.

The train pulled into Union Station and bedlam. The station was festooned with banners. American flags abounded. A fifty-two-piece marching band struck up "Hail the Happy Hero," followed by a spirited rendition of "Pop Goes the Weasel." As Bert descended the steps to the platform a host of schoolgirls ran up to him and began to bombard him with roses. A welcoming committee of dignitaries in frock coats and top hats was waiting to greet him at the top of the ramp. In the forefront stood the mayor, holding a three foot papier-mâché key to the city. Newspaper reporters and photographers swarmed about, and Ben estimated the crowd at close to five thousand souls.

"Mr. Slaughter!" boomed His Honor. "Welcome, sir, to the fair city of San Francisco." His group applauded. "Three cheers for America's hero!" Up went the cheers. "May I present you with the key to the city...."

"Sure."

The key bent in the middle, so spiritedly did the mayor thrust it into his hands.

"Thank ya, Mr. Mayor, and thank ya one and all, ladies, gennelmen, and children o' all ages. It sure is great to be back home to this fair city, though, o' course, home to me is Pile, Nebraska, but to come here back 'mong friends and well-wishers and 'mer'cans o' this great state and even greater country—" Bert started to say.

"Tell us about the assassination!" burst a newspaperman, elbowing forward, pad and pencil at ready. The demand was taken up by other reporters surging forward, elbowing the mayor and the welcoming committee to one side. Bert and

Ben suddenly found themselves wedged in on all sides. Out of nowhere appeared a platoon of policemen wielding nightsticks and pushing forward toward them.

Bert gulped at the sight. "Uh-oh, what's happ'ning?"

"They're going to open the way for us," said Ben.

"Oh."

The policemen did their best and finally succeeded. It took them nearly fifteen minutes to get through the reporters and Bert's army of admirers to the main entrance out onto the sidewalk. People crushed and elbowed one another, struggling to get close enough to the hero to touch him. Autograph books were thrust in his face, hands clutched at his clothing, the fusillade of flowers continued, a crowd twice the size of that inside the station assembled in the street, blocking traffic for half a mile in every direction, and the band played on.

James B. Hume and John Valentine, standing at the rear of the crowd outside the station, could not get within shouting distance of father or son. It wasn't until the helpful police piled them into a hansom cab like two bags of laundry and formed a flying wedge to open the way for their horse that Hume and Valentine were able to follow them at a run for several blocks to Channel Street near Third and their destination, the Crocker House.

The two came puffing up as Bert and Ben emerged from the cab, Bert depositing the key to the city in a convenient trash receptable at the curb.

"Egbert!" boomed Hume.

"James, John, hey, what a great s'prise!"

They pumped hands, Bert slapping them on the back.

"Checking in here?" Valentine asked.

Bert nodded. "Just overnight. Long 'nough to take a bath, loosen up the travel kinks, and get a decent night's sleep in a featherbed. Railroad seats always do crick my neck up somethin' fierce. I'll be haulin' stakes bright and early tomorrow."

"What's the rush?"

"What do you think?" Ben asked grouchily. "The rabbit hunt goes on."

"That one-eyed scum o' the earth's no rabbit, son, and yeah, chasin' him does go on," Bert agreed.

"Can we take time out for a drink and to chat?" asked Hume.

"A drink ya betcha, I'm so dry my throat's cracked. Chat 'bout Wells Fargo and a certain wolf in snake's clothing, no need to mention any names, forget it."

"We'd like you to consider coming back to work," said Valentine bluntly.

"No thanks. Ben here will, but count me out. In spades."

"If you don't mind, I'll speak for myself," said Ben.

"Well, don't think you're taggin' 'long with me. We got all straight on that on the train comin' up the San Joaquin Valley. From now on it's gonna be one to one, which it shoulda been down below, and woulda been if a certain party hadn't'a come taggin' 'long, blunderin' and disruptin' things and slowin' me down to beat the band."

"Ingrate. If I hadn't loaned you money, you'd have had to sleep in an alley for a week."

"You lent me beans! You wouldn't gimme the time o' day; I had to borrow it on the sly."

"Pick my pocket is what you mean—"

"Gentlemen, gentlemen," interposed Hume soothingly, "can we take this inside and perhaps lower it a few decibles?" He winked at Bert. "I'm buying."

"What are we waitin' for?"

In the sedate and dignified surroundings of the Crocker House lobby, under a plaster ceiling cluttered with flying cherubs supported by solid oak beams thirty-five feet high, at a small table on an enormous Smyrna rug, the four of them sat in leather gents' spring-seat easy chairs, alongside potted palms twenty feet tall. James B. Hume dismissed the waiter after he'd served them Hattersly's Bourbon, Bert's "special fav'rite," and proceeded to let out all the stops of his well-rehearsed and convincing argument to persuade Bert to stay on with Wells Fargo. Only because Hume and John Valentine were old friends did Bert have the good manners to listen and not interrupt. Hume cited his long tenure with the company, emphasizing that it was *with the company,* not with Lloyd Tevis. Over the eleven years of Tevis's leadership, he and Bert actually had had little to do with one another. They operated in different, widely separated circles, and regardless of what Bert thought of the man, Tevis had never interfered with his cases. In regard to the recent episode, Bert could scarcely deny that Wells Fargo had essentially funded his sojourn below the border, financed his personal war with Cutler, even to offering ten thousand dollars in ransom money to Herbert Howland as inducement to spare Bert's life.

"Egbert, John and I are your friends," Hume reasoned. "Friendship entails mutual consideration. In light of our friendship we ask you here and now to ignore what happened before you left town, erase it from your mind, and come back to work."

"It's true, you boys are my friends, tried and true friends, and I'm gonna miss ya, but in this game everybody hasta make sacrifices, that's life's way, and that's what I'm gonna hafta make. What you said 'bout me workin' for the comp'ny and not him makes sense, too, but I still can't go back. I don't ever wanta see that face again, and if I don't go back, I don't hafta. When Cutler's dead, and by this hand, I'll take me a long overdue vacation and maybe think 'bout it. Maybe, but right now it's outta the question. 'Sides, he'd never take me back."

"With all that's happened," said Hume, "considering your heroism and the impact it's had on President Grant and others, he'd be stupid to let his obstinacy stand in the way of his common sense. And whatever you think he is, he's not stupid."

"Newspapers'll rake him over the coals," said Valentine.

"I don't care, boys. They can rake him, cook him, or hang him out to dry. It doesn't mean beans to me."

Hume pressed on, but Ben could see and hear in his tone his gradually waning enthusiasm for the effort. He finally gave it up; both he and John Valentine shook hands with father and son, wished them well, and prepared to leave to go back to work.

"What are your plans, Benjamin?" Hume asked.

Ben sighed. "I guess I'll be going back to work." He glared at Bert. "Since nobody else around seems to be in need of my services."

"Glad to hear it," said Hume.

"Half a loaf's better than none," quipped Valentine.

Bert followed both out the revolving door with what Ben decided was a rueful look. Both sipped their drinks in silence, Ben deliberately maintaining his in the hope that Bert's conscience over his decision that they split up would begin pricking him, if only slightly. It did.

"You sore 'cause I wanta go it alone?"

"It's up to you."

"I asked, are ya sore?"

"I'm disappointed you've decided to leave the company."

"What leave? He fired me."

"Hooking up with a new partner might be interesting."

"You're sore."

"As I said, only disappointed." He clucked thinly and without humor. "It's a little ridiculous. I graduated college, I went to work for Wells Fargo, and all through that first year you never let up on me. Insisted this wasn't for me. College graduate, summa cum laude, wasting my brains and my life chasing owlhoots, dodging lead, making next to no money. Why in the world would anybody with all I had to offer choose Wells Fargo?"

"On accounta me..."

"Correct. Only something happened, Bert. After I got that first year under my belt and into the groove, I began to enjoy what I was doing: the satisfaction of the job, mastering the tricks of the trade, the excitement, fascination, the travel, the people we'd meet, the good and bad. For all the hard knocks and drawbacks I've come to really like the challenge of it. Maybe I shouldn't, maybe I *am* 'wasting my education,' but that's the way it's turned out."

"Ben..."

"Let me finish, please. Now you've quit; you don't want me tagging along, so I stay here and go on to another assignment with a new partner. I stick with the job, *the career I chose so I could work with you,* and watch you dump your job, dump me—"

"Son—"

"Please. What's really hard to understand is that you're a man who prides himself on his sense of fairness, and yet what are you doing? You welcomed me aboard your boat, you sailed with me; now you desert and leave me holding the oars.

"Maybe you were right in the first place. My going to work for Wells Fargo, just so we could be together, was a mistake. Maybe now's the time to correct it. I did quit, maybe I should stay quit. Find something else. Does that make sense to you? I can only see one thing wrong with it. I like this job. I love it."

"Aw, for cripes' sakes!"

• • • •

As James Hume confided to John Valentine, Lloyd Tevis had about as much desire to welcome Bert Slaughter back into the fold as he would have had to sit down in the dentist's chair and have all of his teeth yanked. But the onslaught of telegrams from dignitaries north and south of the border, particularly the two from President Grant, dissuaded him from opposing Bert's reinstatement on the company payroll. The president's telegrams *and* the members of the press watching the company like a pack of starving hounds watching a bone about to be tossed into their midst.

Nevertheless, the frigid atmosphere pervading James Hume's office when the hero and his nemesis were brought together for the first time since the Slaughters' return from Mexico was enough to make Ben, Hume, and John Valentine, also present, separately consider raising their coat collars to avoid catching a chill. To add fuel to Hume's fires of persuasion he had brought in a copy of the day's *San*

Francisco Examiner. It lay on his desk, front page up: WELLS FARGO HERO DETECTIVE RETURNS IN TRIUMPH!

Bert offered no reaction to sight of the headline. Tevis almost, but not quite, lifted the corner of his upper lip in a beginning sneer but caught himself in time. Hume cleared his throat, eyeing one, then the other.

"Mr. Tevis, sir, Benjamin has advised me that his father is willing to apologize for his outburst prior to his riding off to Mexico, as well as the phony funeral. He wishes to retract his resignation from the company. Since you, sir, have so graciously agreed to let bygones be bygones and accept Egbert's apology and retraction, I don't see as there's any more to be said on the subject."

"Whattaya mean, 'graciously'!" burst Bert. "And if I gotta 'pologize, he's gotta too! Fair's fair!"

"Now just a moment," said Tevis icily.

"Shut up, Bert," snapped Ben.

"Who you tellin'—"

"I said quiet! An apology is due. Go ahead and make it."

Ben's, Hume's, and Valentine's eyes drilled Bert. Hume's strayed to Tevis. Out of sight under his desk, he crossed his fingers till his knuckles ached, praying that Tevis would not leer at Bert at this critical juncture in the healing process. He did not.

"All right, all right, all right, I 'pologize...."

"Apology accepted," said Tevis quietly.

"You sure better 'cept it!" bawled Bert.

"Shut up, Bert!" exclaimed Ben.

"Neither of us is a fool, Slaughter," said Tevis mildly. "We're both under pressure—different pressures, to be sure—to make peace. Don't think that I don't realize what might happen now that you're back and prepared to accept a new assignment. If and when that renegade pops up, you'll go after him, and the devil with Wells Fargo and your assignment. But I suppose I'll have to tolerate your monkey-shines in that regard, until you've settled things. I do understand your need to avenge the death of your wife. As long as you do your job."

"When did I not? When, tell me!"

"It's not easy to hit two targets at the same time."

"Baloney!"

"Bert..." began Ben, his tone reprimanding.

"All right, all right."

To everyone's astonishment Tevis offered Bert his hand. So surprised was Bert that he shook it before realizing it and, from his expression in reaction, immediately regretted doing so. Tevis rose from his chair.

"If you'll excuse me, I have to get back to work."

Out he walked without another word, leaving Hume's door ajar behind him as usual.

"Very well done, Egbert," said Hume.

"Awwww..."

"Very well," echoed Ben. Valentine nodded.

"It takes a big man to admit he's wrong," said Hume.

"You kiddin'? He had to; newsboys'd never let up on him if he didn't."

"I was talking about you."

"Awwww..."

Bert picked up the paper, eyed the headline with a leer, and began leafing through the pages while Hume got out a bottle of Hattersly's bourbon, specially purchased for the occasion. In the hope, that is, that peace would be restored. He, Valentine, and Ben began talking animatedly. Bert continued to be absorbed in the paper. Browsing through it, he reached the last page. And suddenly gasped and gaped.

"For cripes' sakes! Listen to this! Hey, shut up and listen! Date marked yesterday, Chloride, Ar'zona. You know Chloride, Ben, just north o' Kingston. Listen, the Chloride Miners and Merchants Bank was robbed yesterday and the vault relieved of eleven thousand dollars in cash and silver by five men wearin' bandannas over their faces and last seen ridin' east toward Hackberry. The leader of the gang is described as missin' his right eye."

He slammed the paper to the floor and lurched to his feet. "Let's go, son, we gotta make tracks!"

"Bert..."

Bert didn't hear. As Hume and Valentine stared and Ben gaped, he whirled on his heel, jammed his hat on his head, and pounded out the door. Ben groaned and threw up his hands. Hume, having half risen from his chair, sank back down into it and covered his face with both hands, shaking his head slowly. John Valentine slumped in his chair as limp as a fish, smashing himself in the face with the flat of his hand and eyeing the ceiling through the crack between his first and second fingers.

Epilogue

One month to the day after the attempt on President Lerdo's life, His Excellency traveled to Durango on affairs of state. There a second attempt was made, his assailant firing at him from a rooftop as he rode by in a brougham. Three shots struck the coach, and a fourth slightly wounded Colonel Ignacio Mejía. The would-be assassin was apprehended. Bridget O'Rourke was speedily tried for attempted murder and on the day before Christmas, 1875, was executed by a firing squad in Durango, meeting her death in the city where she had planned Lerdo's.

In 1876, Jose de la Cruz Porfirio Diaz assumed the leadership of a revolution, proclaimed the principle of non-reelection, and defeated the government forces in the battle of Tecoac, on November 16. Diaz was elected president in May of the following year and set about implementing financial and political reforms, the centralization of the government, the reestablishment of public security, the settlement of national debts, and the building of railroads and telegraphs. His rule was stern, sometimes brutal, but he achieved amazing results. With the exception of the four-year term from 1880 to 1884, when the former minister of war, Manuel Gonzalez, held the office, Diaz was president for the next twenty-four years, by virtue of amendments to the constitution to permit his reelection. From 1884 to 1911, he was continuously in office. Under his leadership Mexico enjoyed material prosperity, but it was achieved a the cost of repression and increasing discontent. An incipient revolt led by General Bernardo Reyes in 1903 was quickly crushed, but in 1910, the standard of agrarian revolt was raised; the movement spread swiftly over the country, the government was unable to control the army, and on May 4, 1911, Diaz resigned the presidency and left for Europe. He died in Paris on July 2, 1915, having seen most of the stability which he had brought to his country destroyed.

Renegade by Ramsay Thorne

___#1		(C30-827, $2.25)
___#2	BLOOD RUNNER	(C30-780, $2.25)
___#3	FEAR MERCHANT	(C30-774, $2.25)
___#4	DEATH HUNTER	(C90-902, $1.95)
___#5	MUCUMBA KILLER	(C30-775, $2.25)
___#6	PANAMA GUNNER	(C30-829, $2.25)
___#8	OVER THE ANDES TO HELL	(C30-781, $2.25)
___#9	HELL RAIDER	(C30-777, $2.25)
___#10	THE GREAT GAME	(C30-830, $2.25)
___#11	CITADEL OF DEATH	(C30-778, $2.25)
___#12	THE BADLANDS BRIGADE	(C30-779, $2.25)
___#13	THE MAHOGANY PIRATES	(C30-123, $1.95)
___#14	HARVEST OF DEATH	(C30-124, $1.95)
___#16	MEXICAN MARAUDER	(C32-253, $2.50)
___#17	SLAUGHTER IN SINALOA	(C30-257, $2.25)
___#18	CAVERN OF DOOM	(C30-258, $2.25)
___#19	HELLFIRE IN HONDURAS	(C30-630, $2.25, U.S.A.)
		(C30-818, $2.95, CAN.)
___#20	SHOTS AT SUNRISE	(C30-631, $2.25, U.S.A.)
		(C30-878, $2.95, CAN.)
___#21	RIVER OF REVENGE	(C30-632, $2.50, U.S.A.)
		(C30-963, $3.25, CAN.)
___#22	PAYOFF IN PANAMA	(C30-984, $2.50, U.S.A.)
		(C30-985, $3.25, CAN.)
___#23	VOLCANO OF VIOLENCE	(C30-986, $2.50, U.S.A.)
		(C30-987, $3.25, CAN.)
___#24	GUATEMALA GUNMAN	(C30-988, $2.50, U.S.A.)
		(C30-989, $3.25, CAN.)
___#25	HIGH SEA SHOWDOWN	(C30-990, $2.50, U.S.A.)
		(C30-991, $3.25, CAN.)
___#26	BLOOD ON THE BORDER	(C30-992, $2.50, U.S.A.)
		(C30-993, $3.25, CAN.)
___#27	SAVAGE SAFARI	(C30-995, $2.50, U.S.A.)
		(C30-994, $3.25, CAN.)

WARNER BOOKS
P.O. Box 690
New York, N.Y. 10019

Please send me the books I have checked. I enclose a check or money order (not cash), plus 50¢ per order and 50¢ per copy to cover postage and handling.* (Allow 4 weeks for delivery.)

_____ Please send me your free mail order catalog. (If ordering only the catalog, include a large self-addressed, stamped envelope.)

Name _____

Address _____

City _____

State _____ Zip _____

*N.Y. State and California residents add applicable sales tax.

GREAT ACTION-PACKED WESTERNS
from
L. P. HOLMES

___BRANDON'S EMPIRE (C31-356, $2.95, U.S.A.)
(C31-357, $3.95, Canada)

___CATCH AND SADDLE (C31-354, $2.95, U.S.A.)
(C31-353, $3.95, Canada)

___FLAME OF SUNSET (C31-351, $2.95, U.S.A.)
(C31-352, $3.95, Canada)

___NIGHT MARSHAL (C31-024, $2.95, U.S.A.)
(C31-000, $3.95, Canada)

___PAYOFF AT PAWNEE (C31-349, $2.50, U.S.A.)
(C31-350, $3.25, Canada)

___HILL SMOKE (C31-360, $2.95, U.S.A.)
(C31-361, $3.95, Canada)

___THE PLUNDERERS (C31-069, $2.95, U.S.A.)
(C31-075, $3.95, Canada)

___HIGH STARLIGHT (C31-061, $2.95, U.S.A.)
(C31-062, $3.95, Canada)

WARNER BOOKS
P.O. Box 690
New York, N.Y. 10019

Please send me the books I have checked. I enclose a check or money order (not cash), plus 50¢ per order and 50¢ per copy to cover postage and handling.* (Allow 4 weeks for delivery.)

_____ Please send me your free mail order catalog. (If ordering only the catalog, include a large self-addressed, stamped envelope.)

Name _____
Address _____
City _____
State _____ Zip _____
*N.Y. State and California residents add applicable sales tax.

The King of the Western Novel Is
MAX BRAND

___GUNMEN'S FEUD (C32-049, $2.50, U.S.A.)
(C32-072, $3.25, Canada)

___THUNDER MOON'S CHALLENGE (C32-050, $2.50, U.S.A.)
(C32-319, $3.25, Canada)

___THUNDER MOON STRIKES (C32-074, $2.50, U.S.A.)
(C32-051, $3.25, Canada)

___WILD FREEDOM (C32-769, $2.50, U.S.A.)
(C32-770, $3.25, Canada)

___THE MAKING OF A GUNMAN (C32-412, $2.50, U.S.A.)
(C32-413, $3.25, Canada)

___VALLEY VULTURES (C34-093, $2.75, U.S.A.)
(C34-094, $3.75, Canada)

___TROUBLE IN TIMBERLINE (C32-690, $2.95, U.S.A.)
(C32-691, $3.95, Canada)

___BROTHERS ON THE TRAIL (C34-108, $2.95, U.S.A.)
(C34-107, $3.95, Canada)

___MAN FROM THE WILDERNESS (C32-568, $2.50, U.S.A.)
(C32-569, $3.25, Canada)

WARNER BOOKS
P.O. Box 690
New York, N.Y. 10019

Please send me the books I have checked. I enclose a check or money order (not cash), plus 50¢ per order and 50¢ per copy to cover postage and handling.*
(Allow 4 weeks for delivery.)

_____ Please send me your free mail order catalog. (If ordering only the catalog, include a large self-addressed, stamped envelope.)

Name _____

Address _____

City _____

State _____ Zip _____

*N.Y. State and California residents add applicable sales tax.   12

By the year 2000, 2 out of 3 Americans could be illiterate.

It's true.

Today, 75 million adults... about one American in three, can't read adequately. And by the year 2000, U.S. News & World Report envisions an America with a literacy rate of only 30%.

Before that America comes to be, you can stop it... by joining the fight against illiteracy today.

Call the Coalition for Literacy at toll-free **1-800-228-8813** and volunteer.

Volunteer Against Illiteracy. The only degree you need is a degree of caring.

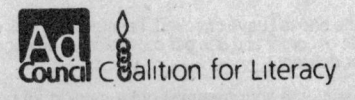

Ad Council Coalition for Literacy

Warner Books is proud to be an active supporter of the Coalition for Literacy.